It's a
Wonderful Life
2060

a novel by George H. Rothacker

Also by George H. Rothacker

FICTION

Singularity 1.0 – The novel
Singularity 2.0 – Finding the Way Back to Humanity
Singularity 3.0 – Sex in Space – The Final Chapter

NON-FICTION

The Diverse Artistic Universe of George H. Rothacker

Table of Contents

Dedicated to my friend and
personal Clarence,
Davld Nelson Wren*

*David is the author of *Ardrossan: The Last Great Estate on the Philadelphia Main Line*

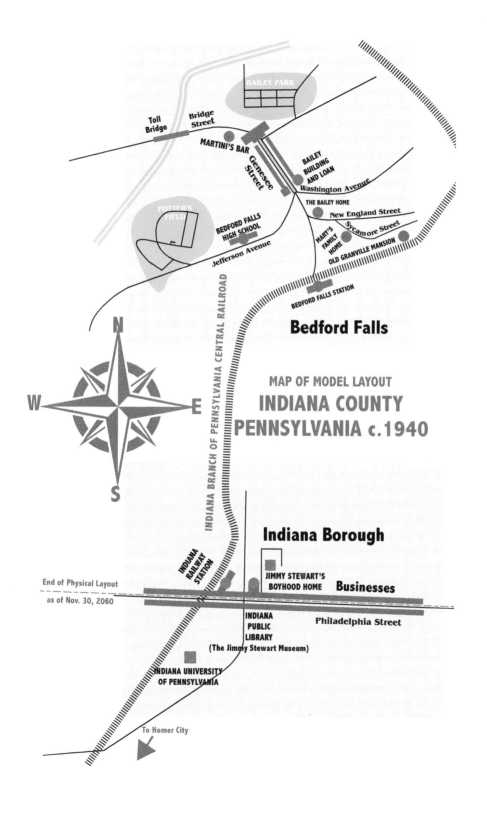

BAILEY PARK

Toll Bridge

Bridge Street

MARTINI'S BAR

Genesee Street

BAILEY BUILDING AND LOAN

Washington Avenue

THE BAILEY HOME

POTTER'S FIELD

BEDFORD FALLS HIGH SCHOOL

New England Street

MARY'S FAMILY HOME

Sycamore Street

OLD GRANVILLE MANSION

Jefferson Avenue

BEDFORD FALLS STATION

Bedford Falls

MAP OF MODEL LAYOUT

INDIANA COUNTY
PENNSYLVANIA c.1940

INDIANA BRANCH OF PENNSYLVANIA CENTRAL RAILROAD

N
W   E
S

Indiana Borough

INDIANA RAILWAY STATION

JIMMY STEWART'S BOYHOOD HOME

Businesses

End of Physical Layout

as of Nov. 30, 2060

INDIANA PUBLIC LIBRARY

Philadelphia Street

(The Jimmy Stewart Museum)

INDIANA UNIVERSITY OF PENNSYLVANIA

To Homer City

Foreword

George and I have been friends for more than 50 years, ever since our school days. He was the one with the active, creative, wacky mind and I was the stable, precise, grounded guy. It made for a good friendship and those traits have now resulted in a perfect pairing of writer and copy editor. Over the past few years we've worked together on four books. His was the harder part.

So when George announced to me that he had started writing a new novel, my ears perked up. After all, his previous books dealt with such futuristic themes as a powerful artificial intelligence striving to understand its place in a world dominated (for the time being) by humans, travel to a planet light-years distant, and communicating with bacteria (really!). And their memorable characters included a woman born with no arms, a humanoid who believes he's a human, and the mysterious *Man in the Yellow Suit.*

When I asked what his latest book was about, George explained that he was working on several storylines, with compelling characters in each, but that there were just too many to properly explore and develop in one book. Familiar with his fertile mind, I encouraged him to just keep writing. We could always edit.

Did I mention that George's original draft took place 100 years from now? He had done his research, so all of the storylines he developed and the situations he described were logical extensions and reasonable extrapolations of current scientific developments and discoveries. However, predicting the future is a risky proposition. What the book needed was something relatable and familiar to the reader of today.

But what was that going to be?

I was delighted when George decided to base his now single storyline on the 1946 movie *It's a Wonderful Life*, as I'm a huge fan of that timeless classic. George's tale revolves around a struggling museum in the year 2060 and a very special model train layout that merges the borough of Indiana, Pennsylvania, with the movie's fictional town of Bedford Falls.

Now get on board, because the train is leaving the station. Next stop: the future! Enjoy the ride.

Manfred Roesler
September, 2021

Chapter One
Fact Checker

Juniper Blakely, 34, a dark-skinned, slightly-built man of Armenian/English descent, awakens at exactly 6:30 AM, as is usual for his weekday schedule. Though he is able to control his sleeping and waking schedule, he finds he's comforted by the implanted pacemaker-type clock that guides his sleep patterns and assures him of maintaining his prescribed number of hours of sleep each night. The clock allows him to effectively plan his days, but he can always change his schedule if the need arises.

Juniper's 32-year-old wife, Leonder, a slender brunette with an attractive blend of features inherited from her Norwegian and Asian parentage, will awaken at 8:00 AM. Her husband is careful to not upset her timetable, just as she respects his, since they both value their independence and share preferences for solitude that seems to balance their marriage.

Juniper showers first, then goes to the kitchen where he finds his breakfast waiting for him. This morning it's a meal of vitamin-enhanced orange juice, plant-based bacon, and eggs provided by organically raised chickens from a nearby farm. He likes to vary his breakfast, and has provided his automated meal system with a list of foods he enjoys that is organized to assure optimal nutrition as well as taste variation.

While having his morning meal, he watches the news on a screen visible to him from all points in the room. He is in control of the channels, but the communication system has optimized his viewing choices over time to cater to his preferences. The volume may be lowered, raised, or muted by Juniper simply thinking about the act and confirming it to himself. He doesn't worry about mistakes that might accidentally interrupt his viewing, since all of his previous errors are accounted for in the process, affording him the luxury of seldom having to correct or make changes to his choices.

Juniper works from home, as do his colleagues at Enstro Technologies. His job is part of a collaborative effort that corrects and adjusts programming errors for communication companies, thus reinforcing security and improving their services. His home office is just a short walk down a hallway from the kitchen, and is basically empty except for a desk. The wall behind the desk is segmented into three screens that enable him to quickly analyze data as it comes in. Juniper is exceptionally suited for multi-tasking, and can concurrently listen to music, watch a game show, and do his work, which keeps him entertained as well as productive.

Juniper's work colleagues are located all over the world. Most speak English, but others have their speech and writing seamlessly translated into English by automated systems that document and store video and text of all interactions between the team members, vendors and communications experts. Artificial Intelligence (AI) is employed to check the accuracy of his work and that of others, which it, at any time, can approve or override as it deems necessary. His interactions on screen, aside from work, are not recorded, so he is free to listen and watch whatever shows or news reports he finds enjoyable without fear of reprimand.

For several weeks, Juniper has been working on an accuracy evaluation of certain news reports issued by information centers around the world. Fact checking has become ever more essential as the world's leaders become more and more influenced by AI. AI provides totally objective information and conclusions for scientists, humanitarians and leaders, allowing them to quickly respond to environmental issues caused by seismic shifts, volcanic disturbances, tornadoes and other destructive weather events. AI also alerts world leaders to local uprisings, reports of espionage from guerilla groups, and terrorist threats issued from rogue space stations, many of which were constructed prior to the 2040 Global Space Accord.

The most pressing issues facing Juniper's group are the subtle variations in contextual information provided by humans in high-level discussions, and the methods AI uses to separate subjective and objective communication. Humans unknowingly often use words and phrases that have multiple meanings that, when translated, can project a meaning other than the one intended. The objective of Juniper's team is to assure that facts remain constant from one communication point to another. As was explained to the team by its human coordinator, conversations are often like a game of "Whisper Down the Lane," in which a story gets inadvertently changed as it passes from one person to another, so that the message delivered to the final person in the group has become radically changed from the one told by the initial person.

Juniper's work schedule is planned out to optimize his efficiency. Therefore, if he begins work at 7:00 AM, he gets a break between 9:30 and 11:00, during which time he can do whatever he likes. Exercise is encouraged, and an online trainer is available who will personally design a program appropriate for an in-home office. Juniper generally will join in for about a half hour, but also often uses the time for one of his hobbies that include gardening, woodworking and a model train layout that he started several years earlier, one that evokes the atmosphere of pre-World War II America.

Nostalgia is a major outlet for many people in the year 2060, since life has changed so radically that men and women have little relationship with their cultural roots. Even looking back just 25 years, the changes have been so extraordinary that it often feels as one might have felt transported back five centuries from the Renaissance to the Dark Ages. Because of the rapid social transformation, organized religion has gained a great boost in membership, since people of the 21st century hunger for community, a concept seldom available in the day-to-day interactions of the modern world.

Lunchtime comes at 1:00 PM, and Juniper has the freedom to eat, interact with his wife, and work on his hobbies until 2:00. His workday normally ends at 4:00 PM, but sometimes is shorter, or can extend long into the evening, depending on the urgency of his tasks.

Leonder also works from home, in a pottery studio where she throws bowls on an antique potter's wheel. She was educated as an engineer, but her skills were limited, so she was encouraged to find a productive endeavor more suited to those skills. Leonder had little education in the arts, but she understood mechanics, so chose to give pottery a try. In the process she discovered that she was better at the craft than she had anticipated. She also found that she could expand her output to include personalized cups, jugs, ornamental tiles, vases and sculptures. Since income wasn't a factor, she was able to spend as much time as she liked on any one piece, and found that friends and acquaintances would gladly pay her well for "replacements" of their existing machine-made crockery, dinnerware, pots, and planting containers.

Needless to say, their own home's interior is decorated with brightly colored tiles, as is the exterior of the house, and it's remarkably distinctive. Juniper is somewhat envious of his wife's success, and wishes that he could spend more time on his model railroad, recreating the scenic beauty of the trestles, train yards, saw mills and villages that once dotted the American landscape.

Despite his regrets, Juniper finds his job satisfying, often imagining it as a large jigsaw puzzle missing only a few pieces, with his job and those of his colleagues being to find each errant piece and place it in its rightful spot to reveal the complete picture of an issue. Unfortunately, Juniper is finding that the number of missing pieces keeps multiplying, with breaches developing more quickly than can be managed, and with more workers like him needed to protect the world from phishers and spammers. To compound the problem, the sophistication of the intelligence guiding systems is making it nearly impossible for human programmers to understand which alterations are safeguards and which are Trojan horses designed to trick humans into believing their efficacy. Juniper often feels that the world should be more secure than ever, while in reality all nations seem only a hair's breadth away from collapse.

Human leaders know that "reliability" of information isn't a new problem. It's existed for centuries, but is more troublesome to leaders now since there is so much more information to be analyzed. Ultimately, scientists and philosophers agree that the world's problems have become more "human" in nature, as truths and facts have become more evident and predictions more accurately proven.

Few of the answers provided by science are necessary for human life and, despite their accuracy, there consistently remains a 50%-50% balance between beliefs in religious and spiritual answers, and scientific ones. This ratio remains constant even as scientific discoveries are being utilized by nearly all of the world's population.

Juniper thinks of this late one evening as he faithfully populates the train layout of his 1940s miniature universe, molding and painting 1:87 scale (3.5 mm to 1 foot) figurines sawing wood, climbing ladders and thumbing for rides from drivers in pre-WWII cars. His thoughts are far away as he divorces himself from the world in which he lives and works. The world in which he pretends to live is guided by false memories that ignore the plagues, mistruths and hypocrisies of the past, no doubt in an effort to cope with the hard realities of the modern world, in which there are no excuses, no falsehoods, and no hope for a better future.

"Leonder has her pottery, and I have my trains," he thinks. Both are means of escape, while others turn to religion or hacking into the world's computer networks. "Deliver us from evil, please!" he raises his head in prayer, before turning off his mind to focus on a tiny figure of a farmer in overalls that he's painting with a small brush. The man is seated on a bale of hay, with folded arms and one foot on a bag of seed. He is looking upwards to a point above the horizon, perhaps at a sunset, or dreaming of a better life. "How fortunate you are, my little man," Juniper thinks as he places his completed sculpture on the train layout next to a wagon with two children playing beside it.

The lights turn off as Juniper leaves the room and returns upstairs to his wife, who's already asleep, and welcomes the oblivion he will enjoy before tomorrow's dawn.

Chapter Two
Movie Night

Once a month, Juniper and Leonder gather with friends at Falon Justy's pod, a pre-cast and fitted form of housing located in the Erran Heights suburb of Crestoria, a community incorporated in southern California. Crestoria was established in 2037 as a model for other communities, and was built in the previously barren Mojave region as technology enabled the region to support agriculture, manage rainfall and reinforce the fault line that had threatened the population of the area.

The reason for the gatherings is "Movie Night," at which a group of twelve neighbors attend viewings of classic movies of the twentieth century. The most popular films feature famous actors of the late 1930s to the 1960s, with the exception being certain disaster films of the '70s and '80s that all members of the group find hilariously funny.

Falon is part of the team that works with Juniper at Enstro Technologies, with his job being a "parameter specialist," a human who guides the limits of accuracies permitted by AI to be enforced in establishing the rules of businesses working in unity throughout the world. He and his wife, Astra, moved into Erran Heights two years before Juniper and Leonder and introduced them to their friends, all of whom had relocated from other communities to test the viability of a technologically developed environment suitable for human habitation.

Erran Heights is unlike most other communities in that it is designed for efficiency and simplicity of operation while providing an environment geared to human comfort and community. Nothing is "stick-built" in Erran Heights. All pod locations are planned, as is the future development of every market, store, park, and entertainment center. As many of the residents say about living there, "There is no *old* in Erran Heights."

That same standard applies to the residents, whose ages range from 23 to 45. Both the Blakelys and the Justys are in their early 30s, with their group of friends in the community averaging 35 years of age.

Falon Justy was born and raised in rural West Virginia, with his childhood reminiscent of many aspects of life that date back to the 1980s. He grew up in a close family spanning several generations, in which the oldest member spun stories of hopping freight trains at the age of nine or ten, taking off on long bike rides without a helmet or other protective gear, and swimming in non-environmentally clean creeks and not coming home until after dark. He also grew up watching old movies on television monitors with his grandfather, who as a child was introduced to them by his parents.

At his current age of 35, Falon is less familiar with the musical and film stars of today than he is with Clark Gable, Jean Harlow, Humphrey Bogart and Rita Hayworth.

Nostalgia is important to those living in a sterile community, and in the same way that Falon loves old films and Juniper is addicted to old trains, most of the citizens of Erran Heights embrace some form of pre-21st century genre, game, book series, craft, or technology.

Tonight's movie is *The Maltese Falcon*, starring Humphrey Bogart as Sam Spade. To add to the experience, Falon recently purchased a 35mm Universal projector online and acquired a print of that film, along with prints of several other classic movies.

The projector and film add to the twelve 2010-era theater seats he purchased that allow viewers to lay back and enjoy popcorn made on a 1960s popcorn popper. Each film night, Falon gives a briefing on the director, writer and cinematographer, along with the actors in the film.

To create the theater, Falon had to receive a special variance for the addition from the community, and has since added theatrical draping, a podium, and an adjustable viewing screen, all to enhance the retro experience.

"Sometimes the film breaks, and I have to splice it together and we have to wait for the fix," Falon tells each person who has been invited for the first time. "This isn't always a smooth process. Bulbs are hard to find, and we can't always determine the quality of the film….but that's part of the experience.

"Some people just don't get it," he confessed to Juniper recently. "They ask why I do it this way, when it's so much easier to dial the film up digitally. After the evening is over, a few get it. Others never do. They are stuck in the world of today and can't transport themselves back in time."

"I understand it, Falon," answered Juniper. "I think some of us are hardwired with the need for it; we can learn to look back. But some can only look forward, and appreciate the present and the next new thing.

"I've noticed that, especially at work, and sometimes have a hard time communicating why some of the decisions made are just plain wrong, even when I have no information to back up my viewpoint."

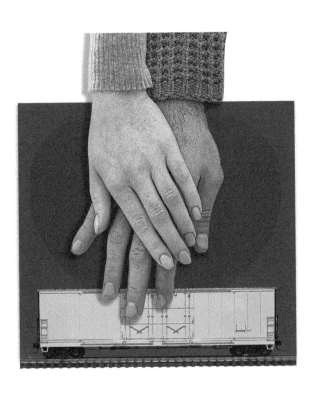

Chapter Three
Romantic Love

Except for his model railroad layout, Juniper Blakely finds his life less thrilling than he dreamed as a teen it would be. Though he believes that he loves his wife, he finds their marriage boring. They still have sex an average of once a month, but children seem too great a burden for either of them to consider. They've tried spicing up their sex life by bringing toys and robots into their bedroom. The first time the robot was male and the second time it was female. It was kind of fun at first, but then it proved embarrassing. Leonder wasn't comfortable with Juniper watching her having *too* good a time with the male robot, and she found it disgusting to watch him slurping and pawing the female bot and acting like a schoolboy in heat. After those two attempts, they never tried a bot threesome again, yet each, alone, has rented one on occasion. It may be that humans prefer the sequestered act, and sex with a partner who doesn't judge, fart, or show indifference.

When working on the railroad, creating trees or crafting stations, Juniper thinks about women a lot, mostly conjuring up actresses of an earlier age... women who acted in the same genre of classic films that the couple watches at Falon Justy's pod. A favorite of both couples is *Picnic*, with William Holden and Kim Novak. Leonder finds Holden to be the sexiest man on the planet, especially in the way he dances with Novak in the picnic scene. All of the men at Movie Night find Novak not only gorgeous, but sexy beyond belief. The women find her phony... a "wooden" actress. But women don't see things the same as men. The men all admire Holden's command in the film and the way he seductively draws Novak closer as the heat turns up in the final segment of the picnic scene.

For the third viewing of the film, two other couples have joined the group and it leads to a discussion of the actors and actresses of the past, and how they measure up against those in contemporary films. All of the couples agree that the characters of the past seem more believable than the ones appearing in the films of today, even though the acting has gotten better.

"That makes no sense. If the acting's better, why shouldn't they be more believable?" questions Oliver Burns, a regular guest at the viewings.

"I don't know," says Juniper. "Maybe I just don't like the characters they play as much.

"Let's talk about *On the Waterfront*," he continues. "Was it a better film than most movies nowadays, or is it just that it was the first of its kind, setting the stage for many others like it? Or does it matter?"

"I think it matters," answers Oliver. "Films, like books and songs, need some age behind them. There are many crummy 1940s films, and many bad actors and actresses, but Brando was fantastic in that one because he was one of the first to inject realism into his part. It remains genuine even more than 100 years later."

"Who are your favorite actresses?" asks Cynthia, a new member of the group. She came with her husband Ben, who also works with Juniper.

Ben answers, "Well, you know mine, Cynthia!"

"No, Ben, I know of many. Who is your top pick?"

"Can it be a *current* actress?"

"Of course."

"Then I pick Silvid Keansley."

"You like her?" questions Cynthia.

"She seems real to me, a little the way Novak was in *Picnic.* She's hot but subtle.... dreamy...and I love her Australian accent."

Tom, another newbie, chimes in, "I know what you mean about Keansley, Ben. I love her overbite."

"I love the way she looks at men... like she adores them," says Falon.

"I have one you may not have ever known about like that," says Juniper. "Caterina Valente!"

"Who the hell's that?" exclaims Oliver.

"You've got to look her up online. She's got that thing Tom said about Keansley. She could make a man feel that he was the only guy in the room."

"What was she in?" asks Tom.

"Mostly foreign musicals. Looked a little like Audrey Hepburn, but she was also a great singer and dancer and played the guitar. She appeared on a lot of the 1960s variety shows – like the Dean Martin, Perry Como and Danny Kaye shows. I've watched her over and over again as she sings with them...to them... and you can watch them each falling in love with her. She spoke six languages and could sing in eleven. She..."

"Okay," interrupts Cynthia. "Somebody tell me their favorite actor."

"I have to go with Holden," reaffirms Leonder. "But I'll also go with Jon Peter Davis."

"That's an interesting choice," answers Cynthia. "He hasn't been around in years. Didn't he get killed, or die of something horrible?"

"Yes," answers Leonder. "He was in a bad hovercraft accident and died weeks later. Lost half of his face and an arm in the process. I didn't have to listen to a word he said; I was just mesmerized by him."

"Well, guys, I know she's not mesmerized by me," says Juniper with a laugh.

"I was when we first met," replies Leonder.

"Wow!" says Ben. "Mesmerized by him!"

"Yes, Ben! Do you remember where we met, Juniper?"

"No, but I remember when I first saw you. You were with this guy at a job fair. Either you or he was taking applications. I was looking for work at another booth and wandered over, but you were chatting with an applicant.

"I even remember what you were wearing. Your outfit was black and yellow, and your shoes were black short heels with large white dots."

"Whoa, Juniper!" says Alex, another guest. "What kind of underwear was she wearing?"

"She was just so cute, and approachable. The fellow she was talking to had a big smile, and she kept trying to read the brochure to him, and he just kept looking at her and smiling."

"How come I never heard that story?" says Leonder.

"It never came up till now. I think we actually met a few days later by accident. I was leaving a store... and you walked by and dropped a package. I picked it up for you."

"That's right," says Leonder. "I thanked you and you started to leave..."

"I was afraid you knew that I had seen you before at the job fair and that you'd think I was stalking you."

"No, I didn't remember you. But then you stopped and turned and asked me if I liked Led Zeppelin. I thought it so strange, like how could you know?"

"The package you dropped. It was a biography of Jimmy Page. The title wasn't on the cover, but I was a big fan...all these years later."

"You just kept talking about him and the band," says Leonder.

"I figured the longer I talked, the longer you would stay and not try to escape."

"I was fascinated. Of course, I hadn't read the book since I just bought it, but you knew his whole history... replacing somebody with the Yardbirds."

"The bassist, Paul...something....Smith."

"Yep! Samwell-Smith," says Leonder. "I remember."

"Then I asked you if your favorite color was yellow and your mouth dropped open. It was a guess, because of the dress you were wearing at the job fair."

"You guessed right, but didn't tell me how you knew. Was it magic?"

"Yes, it was!" says Juniper with a smile.

There is a moment of quiet, and then Cynthia looks from one person to another, and says, "My God! That was almost as romantic as the dance scene in *Picnic.*"

"It was," says Leonder quietly, and in that moment she realizes that she is still in love with Juniper.

Chapter Four
A Model World

In the summer of 2000, while he was on vacation in Zurich, Frederik Braun stopped into a model train store and came up with an idea that became the "Miniatur Wunderland," the largest tourist attraction in Hamburg, Germany.

By 2020, the exhibit had reached its final construction phase. At that point it contained 1,300 trains, more than 100,000 moving vehicles, 500,000 lights, and 400,000 human and animal figurines on a landscape that covered nearly 25,000 square feet. To fit everything into that space, Braun and his twin brother Gerrit created the layout in HO scale, beginning with the construction of the fictitious city of Knuffingen and expanding the layout to include sections for Central Germany, the Alps, Austria, Hamburg, America, Scandinavia, Switzerland and Italy.

Despite its planned completion in 2020, construction continued over the next 20 years, adding sections for Central America and the Caribbean, Asia, Africa, England and The Netherlands. Today, special features include a simulated daily routine of twilight, night and day repeated every 15 minutes, a firefighting operation in Knuffingen that also repeats every quarter hour, and more than 300 visitor-controlled actions that include the start of a mine train operation, a goal scored in a soccer stadium, and a spacecraft leaving the earth from Cape Canaveral, complete with a fiery blastoff and the breaking away of the structure supporting the booster rockets.

In June of last year, Juniper and Leonder took time off from their jobs to visit Hamburg and the model city, which required several days to view in its entirety. While there, they took a behind the scenes tour of the workshops, and the digital control center reportedly updated every few years to accommodate new and experimental technologies not yet incorporated into real world scenarios. A special section has been built that provides a glimpse into the years ahead; it includes hovercars, AI-controlled damming systems, and robot-managed factories that create new miniature products in real time from raw materials: trees, figurines, and structures shipped to new areas of the layout without human intervention. What started out as a railroad layout has become a miniature testing ground for real-world industrial processes. Since tests are conducted in a controlled environment, and in miniature form, costs are comparatively low and the tests provide little threat to humans, except that they reveal possibilities for similar processes that definitely will affect the future of humans, their work habits, and their reduced value in many industrial operations.

Over the last several years, similar miniature worlds have popped up in Beijing, Chengdu, Tokyo, and Sydney, but none of them have yet been able to match the range and complexities of the Hamburg exhibition, which has attracted more than 130 million visitors since its opening in 2010.

As Juniper works on his own small 1940s-themed railway, he imagines the possibilities for a miniature wonderland in America, and has communicated with other enthusiasts about taking on such a project. He envisions his miniature world to be based on railroad history, extending from the steam era into diesels and the decline of passenger traffic due to the rise of the superhighways and airline travel. His concept is fueled by the desire for simpler times, but with the intention of using miniature technology to replace many of the burdensome and repetitive tasks of creating the quantities of miniaturized figures, trees, rock formations, automobiles and buildings required to populate the vast landscapes he envisions.

In his head, he understands the anomaly of reducing the input of human activity that he and other modelers enjoy in order to create the vast historic landscape he imagines. But the temptation is quite irresistible, and he feels his actions are justified because it will allow many more to watch the activities of America's past come alive in miniature towns and cities throughout the heartland, on farms, in factories, and on the shores of fishing villages filled with wooden schooners, crew boats, ferries and tugs.

Many with whom he communicates are resistant to the task, reminding Juniper of the Zen-like concentration that goes into creating each tree, rock ledge and park bench.

Juniper understands their reasoning, but he is sometimes frustrated by the meticulousness of each task, and imagines more being done than he can manage in his free time.

This is not to say that Juniper is hypocritical. It's just that he cannot view those painstaking, solitary tasks as sufficient enough to fulfill his dreams.

Through a work connection, Juniper reaches out by electronic mail to the urban planners of the 100 most undervalued cities in the United States to see if they might be interested in such a project. Surprisingly, among the top 10 are Philadelphia, Baltimore, St. Louis and Pittsburgh. In his presentation he provides actual figures of property values, high school graduation levels, lifestyle rankings, and the probability for the growth of tourism in the targeted regions. He also provides a summary of the tourism growth of the cities in the world that have supported projects of this kind, compared to those that have attracted visitors with theme and amusement parks similar to those of Disney, Universal Studios and Epcot, as well as fantasy parks that provide virtual reality adventures like Next World, Ballinshade and Mind Xpander.

Within days of Juniper's outreach, he receives thirty-one email responses asking for additional information. City planners in Providence, Rhode Island, New Haven, Connecticut, and Pittsburgh, Pennsylvania, requests a visual contact call as well as more information.

As a "truth finder," Juniper has no difficulty locating up-to-the-minute data about cities that the local governments don't have, and he estimates costs based on robotic versus human time, human economic impact, and employment figures for the first and second phases of a planned startup. He also takes video clips of his own miniature railroad to point out some features that might be duplicated and enhanced upon in future projects.

He forwards the requested materials by electronic mail to all of his contacts, and sets up video appointments with the city planners of the three cities that have shown the most interest. To prepare for the meetings, he and Leonder have spent several hours setting up cameras at strategic points on Juniper's 20' x 25' train layout. They also have installed an overhead camera that shows the layout from above, which Juniper can switch to as needed. His main screen shows him to the left side of the nose of a 4-8-8-4 steam locomotive with the Pennsylvania Railroad keystone on the center-plate.

He has also collected clips of videos of "Wéixíng shìjiè," the Beijing version of "Miniatur Wunderland" that features scenic highlights from Shanghai to Bejing, Kumming to the Silk Road, the journey from Chengdu to Xi, and segments showing the reproduction of The Ghan train that takes visitors on a magical trip from Adelaide in southern Australia, the land of kangaroos, emus and koalas, through the outback to Darwin in the north, the home of cassowaries and clownfish.

Juniper has also produced a rough draft of the stages of the envisioned project, each starting in the targeted city and branching out to all corners of the country. Included are National Parks, historic battlefields, and places marking unique milestones in the history of America occurring during the greatest era of rail travel.

Knowing that costs and benefits will be of more interest than featured sites and events, Juniper has been able to use his company's computers to estimate tourist and local traffic for each phase of the program, and created a growth chart of hotels, restaurants and collateral businesses affected by the installation, overlaying projected revenue-to-cost estimates over a ten-year period. By accessing data of other miniature worlds in operation, he is able to enumerate the advantages for each host city, were it to take on the project. All of this is also backed up by statistics proving a growing focus on "nostalgia," as witnessed by the sale of T-shirts, books, films, games, and images of past heroes, as the growth of technology has desensitized humans to the fantasies of the future and the realities of the modern world.

Juniper's first video meeting has been scheduled with the planning committee of New Haven, Connecticut, which was curious, but not convinced of the project's worth and somewhat astounded at the $575 million price tag for the start-up, and the $1.5 billion additional dollars needed to be raised over ten years to grow the project. Their hesitation is based on the fact that the initial cost is twice the amount they had budgeted, and would be difficult to sell to the city council, even with the projection that the city would recover the start-up revenues within three years of the exhibition's opening.

Juniper reminds the planning commission that New Haven will not be the major focus of the market for this project, and that the first phase will encompass New York City, laying claim to Broadway, Rockefeller Center and the Great White Way, Harlem and its Renaissance, Brooklyn and its Dodgers, the Bronx and its Yankees, as well the city's rich heritage of intrigue and struggle during Prohibition, the Great Depression and World War II.

After an exhaustive meeting, it is apparent that New Haven is not prepared for such a project, though its rail connection to New York City is most enticing.

Juniper's next meeting is with the planners and tourism managers of

Providence, Rhode Island. Their railroad dates back to 1835 with a station built by the Boston and Providence Railroad at India Point. It has served the northeast corridor for 225 years and provides service to New York City and Washington, D.C. All in the meeting are enthused with the project, but they are a small state and the cost seems high, as the city has little room to grow, or to even house the scale of the intended project.

Pittsburgh is the last on the shortlist of video meetings, and Juniper has spent a good amount of time exploring the city's rail history. Though headquartered in Philadelphia, the Pennsylvania Railroad (PRR), founded in 1846, became the foremost railroad company in the United States, with Pittsburgh its most important hub, as its tracks wandered through Ohio and Indiana, and across Illinois to Chicago. Pittsburgh has depended on its rail service since its only two waterways flow north to south, and there is no access by ships to provide transport to the major cities, including Philadelphia, New York and Baltimore, and the western states.

Pittsburgh has come far during the past century and early in the 21st century was named by the Metropolis Guide as "one of the most livable cities in the world." As the city became deindustrialized in the mid-1900s, it upped its game and transformed itself into a hub for health care, education and technology, and became the sixth-best area for job growth in the United States as it entered the 21st century.

The video conference with city planning personnel grew to a group of 23 individuals from business and government entities, all of whom were receptive to the idea of the miniature railroad marking Pittsburgh as a major center of industry in the nation. As ideas were thrown out for discussion, the planners wanted to know what it would take to decrease the timeline for Phase One to get the small railroad into operation. Tech companies asked how they could assist with construction, offering financing, robotic help and engineers.

The city was willing to provide historians, and the colleges to provide paid interns for layout design, planning and construction. The art community also had a representative who saw the potential for new miniature sculptures and art installations throughout the landscape that could be transformed into large scale for the city.

Though no final approvals were given at the meeting, a counterproposal was promised within a month.

"Please do not offer this project to any other city before we get back to you," said Regis Delsey, the head of city planning, before the online meeting ended.

Juniper marvels at his good fortune, thinking that he has probably approached the city at just the right time in its history. It appears that the facts he'd compiled were not necessary for the acceptance of the ideas in his proposal. If anything, New Haven may have had more to gain from the project than Pittsburgh. The excitement seemed to come from a bit of financial wizardry, and a decent amount of city pride, but mostly from a large dose of human enthusiasm in challenging Chicago, New York, Philadelphia and Los Angeles to become a leading city in many areas of development, and to profit from the venture by making a significant mark on its history and its vision... and transferring the dreams created in miniature form, gradually raising the scale into a full-sized section of the Pittsburgh they knew the city could one day become.

For Juniper, the "romance" of the project out-shines the realties, if only enough to help him realize his passion in a way quite impossible for him to completely grasp. Looking back to the 1939 New York World's Fair, and its Futurama exhibition that took people on a miniature journey of life into a full-scale section of the city in the future, he sees that the only way he can define his journey is to imagine it, and the only way for others to experience it is to show them that it already exists.

Chapter Five
Is it Possible?

*A*s *a child I dreamed of such an adventure, one that would take me back in time to a world intuitively understood – a world absent from my own. The world I lived in then was one of virtual reality. There were no motors in my childhood – no gears, no magnetic switches, no wrenches or pulleys.*

I thought I knew no differently, as I matured and gained responsibilities, but the ghost of what I remembered lay beyond yet another horizon. As I became employed and got married, I entrenched myself in the technology of the 21st century. But I could separate my values, and compartmentalize the working world from my dreams set in some earlier era. At times I thought I knew where I was headed, and pushed for it despite a longing that sent me to the lower floor of the pod that Leonder and I shared, and into a world of which she understood little. Waiting for me when the lights came on was Number 58, a steam engine built in 1886 and still active at the start of World War II, an era when the Rocky Mountains and the Rio Bravo were vibrant with the sounds of engines, car horns and grinding metal.

––––––––––––––

In 1942, Gunnison, Colorado, situated at the mouth of the Ohio Creek Expansion in the foothills of the Rocky Mountains, was a historic mining town, and held the record for the coldest city in the contiguous United States. Industries included Swift Company meat packers and Notlaw Lumber. The sidewalks were still mostly made of wood and most of the roads were gravel. Buildings on the main street included D.S. Hyman and Co. Wholesale Liquor Dealers, the Pearl Laundry & Bath Rooms, and Edible Grain Produce. Landmark buildings were made of brick or stone and included the LaVeta Hotel, Mt. Gothic Tomes & Reliquary, the Gunnison Arts Center, and Gunnison Bank and Trust.

Juniper's train layout takes up most of the ground floor of his pod, which had previously been divided into two rooms. The space is small in contrast with other private model railroads he has seen online or visited, but his artistry is superb and the accuracy of his portrayal of Gunnison has been hailed by railroad aficionados and historians alike for the intense research and skill incorporated into the creation of the miniature landscape.

Based on the response from the Pittsburgh Planning Commission, Juniper delves further into that city's past and incorporates more detail into a plan that would most benefit the Steel City. If the project is deemed feasible, he will be able to resign his job and devote his time fully to his hobby, a dream he never thought possible.

Four days later, Juniper gets a call inviting him to present online before a larger group, which includes the mayor and members of the City Council, in just two weeks. Because of the "heads up" prior to the invitation, Juniper has reached out to John Sayre, a contact he met on the Model Railroading

Network, who is the head of M-Bots, a microbotics firm that provides trackless magnetic guidance systems for assembly line operations. Sayre, a model railroad enthusiast, had written an article about having created a more lifelike performance for model cars and trucks populating his HO scale layout, and showed in a video how his miniature vehicles accelerated, turned and braked realistically in the same way that his engines do on tracks.

Most model railroaders of the 21st century incorporate moving vehicles into their layouts, but Sayre's cars are stunning in that they can switch lanes, automatically stop at traffic lights and yield to other vehicles when approaching a highway, without manual input or special programming. Many HO-scale cars measure only 1-1/2 inches in length, and the operating systems usually fit within an area less than 1 inch x 3/4 inches with a maximum height of only 3/8 inch. Juniper approaches Sayre and tells him of the Pittsburgh project by asking the question, "Can you make HO-scale 'people' walk or run?"

Sayre thinks for a moment, and says, "I don't really know. We haven't tried...but I suppose it's possible."

This leads Juniper to question Sayre about scale and how the tiny trackless vehicles are created.

"Our robots make smaller robots capable of making even smaller robots until we get down to the perfect size for the task at hand," says Sayre. "We already create microbots that are less than .078 inches long, but usually their functions are limited. Building a walking person would require a bit more sophistication."

"Here's where I'm coming from," says Juniper enthusiastically. "It's great to see the engine chugging along and the cars uncoupling and regrouping. It's even more exciting when there are vehicles moving on the road, but what if we could populate a layout with people walking, running and interacting?"

"Whoa," says Sayre. "That sounds extremely complex and expensive... and far beyond anything we can do at the moment."

"Yes," answers Juniper. "But it 'might' be possible."

"Someday... perhaps," says Sayre.

"Okay... so you create a team of tiny robots who scale down a larger robotic person and provide the person with movable parts...like any other robot...and you cover each one with a flexible sheathing... and add clothes..."

"Wait, Juniper!" exclaims Sayre, stopping him in mid-sentence. "How many of these would you need, and how many configurations? It's unimaginably complicated, and as I said... expensive. Just creating a prototype could cost millions since it means training smaller and smaller robots to perform an astronomical number of complex tasks."

"But that's what you do, isn't it?" answers Juniper naively.

The two are quiet for about ten seconds, then Juniper asks. "What if you developed them for complex surgical procedures?"

"What? HO-scale human-looking people?"

"They wouldn't have to look human... for medical purposes."

"We already have robots for that," answers Sayre.

"Then why can't we dress one up and see what it looks like, and how it could work?"

"That's like taking a rhinoceros and making it into mouse," says Sayre.

"Can I see what you've already got?" asks Juniper. "And then we can see what it would take to transform one little rhinoceros into a human-looking rhinoceros?"

"You're asking a lot," says Sayre.

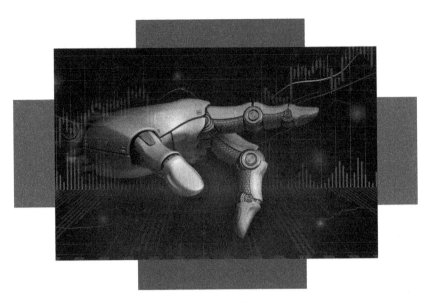

Chapter Six
Microbots

John Sayre has two passions: robotics and model railroading. Over the past 22 years, he has kept them separate, in that the systems he incorporates into his 1950s O-gauge layout use little of the technology introduced in the 21st century. His switches are electromechanical and every building, tree and mountain is created in the identical manner it would have been done a hundred years ago.

He scribes boards into the basswood siding of each house he crafts with an X-Acto saw, and creates trees from dowels, small branches and lichen. And he stays true to the materials and tools of the history of the art by handcrafting every bush, rock, person and animal that occupies space on his miniature railroad layout.

John Sayre is not a Buddhist, but his methods adhere to rules that are monastic, and consistent with the beliefs of model railroaders long gone. Ease is not something he strives for, since accomplishments for him are measured by the dedication to the task, beyond the achievement of a goal. Process is purpose, and contentment is found in hard work and diligence to honorable tasks and values not necessarily observed in the field of microbotics.

As the head of M-Bots, he is guided by the principles of economics, efficiency, and adherence to practical solutions from proven methods learned over time.

On his train layout, the finished product means nothing without the observance of the processes of his predecessors, whereas in his job he is always searching for the future of "what if," "how," and "can this be possible" every day in each new method at his disposal.

Juniper's challenge to create miniature robotic people weighs on Sayre's mind as he works under a magnifier aging bricks on a Birds Eye factory building modeled after the frozen food giant's headquarters in Chicago in the 1920s. He has always attempted to separate what he does for a living from who he is and where he lives inside himself – a different place and a time existing long before his birth. But now he realizes that he cannot avoid the merging of both sides of his personality with the products he creates.

After completing a brick wall at the entrance to the plant and adding period signage to the factory walls, he leaves his basement and returns upstairs to his home office. As he approaches, hidden light sources switch on and a bank of computers greets him as he sits down and instructs his workstation to locate the latest information on his company's microbotic development plans. As of a month ago, several microbots had been teamed together to construct a lightweight truss system from metallic micro-lattice to test the viability of using the netting as an alternative to steel for full-scale bridge construction. By scaling the bridge down in size, the engineers determined the integrity of micro-lattice for new uses as well as a lightweight substitute for failing bridges. The model also qualified the materials as appropriate for structures such as skyscrapers that are exposed to stressful seismic and climatic conditions.

Microbots are generally constructed differently than biologically engineered nanobots. They can be manufactured as small as .078 of an inch in length, but because of their small size their use is limited to the replication of tasks rather than for multi-operation purposes. In order to create miniature people at 1:87 scale (HO-gauge), microbots must duplicate several human actions and be of comparable strength to life-sized robots. At a scale no larger than 1:44, a similar size to an O-gauge person, a robotic figure would measure approximately two inches in height. Microbots of this size would need to have fully functioning arms and legs and sufficient brainpower to machine, assemble, paint and accessorize multi-jointed HO-gauge operational replicates, as well as to install and connect the flexible circuits to each tiny brain.

Sayre has no doubt that his engineers can create the O-gauge robotic work crew, because his company already has the technology and materials necessary to form the 1:44 scale robots. But as an owner, Sayre can't develop a suitable economic reason to use his factory for the creation of prototypes narrowly defined by his own personal interests as a hobbyist, rather than for a more marketable concept to address the needs of humankind.

Sayre leaves his workstation and returns to his basement and the Birds Eye factory he's been detailing. While painting with a small brush, and using his X-Acto knife to scrape and roughen surfaces, he makes note of the movements he uses in each of the tasks and imagines what it would be like if the building were several times the size of "O" scale. Though the amount of surface area would be greater, the repetitive tasks would be easier to accomplish, with fewer motions required. Using several robots would quicken the process, and over time the AI workforce would figure out how to accomplish all of the required tasks more efficiently.

When Sayre is done with the building, he goes back upstairs to his computer, logs in and opens his robotic sketch pad and begins a design of hand movements, simplifying the points and digits to a number that will allow for micro robots to duplicate the tasks he performed on the Birds Eye factory, including the painting of exterior lamps, door handles and window pulls. When complete, he renders the sketched movements into a 3D virtual animation and plays it back in real time to test the movements. He then sketches an arm with an elbow and a rotating shoulder joint. And then he connects it to a body that will house the brain containing a protruding optical antennae and the high-torque direct drive motors necessary for flexible movement and lift. Though the systems are available for equipment as large as O-gauge, there are no motors yet available for the 1:44-scale human replicates. By simplifying the movements, he is able to create the illusion of walking, running and interactions of humans without the sophistication needed by the O-gauge sized robots used for the creation of the HO-gauge humans.

The brains of the larger workers will need to be fairly sophisticated, so Sayre finds an existing chip powerful enough to perform and learn tasks necessary to create the smaller-sized replicates who will have no need to hear or see; they need only follow a program of wirelessly transmitted movements from signals outside of their bodies. These experiments will lead to the building of "O," a virtual robot with collapsible legs and a rolling tread system, simplified hands and arms, and optical sensors. "O," though looking nothing like a human, will be capable of many, if not all, of the tasks performed by larger, full-scale robots with the only difference being that the "O" robots will be created in miniature form.

Uses could range from repairs on computer hardware and circuitry to the reconstruction and repair of delicate bones and organs in humans, birds and animals, and the construction of scaled-down prototypes of aircraft, automobiles, space stations, launch pads and supply chain operation centers, at a cost far less than the production of an identical full-sized prototype or system.

Sayre also knows that, once manufactured, a team of "Os" will also be capable of creating hundreds of thousands of animated miniature human clones that, when painted and accessorized, will add a sense of "life" to Juniper's proposed Pittsburgh project.

With his sketches rendered into animated videos, Sayre contacts the head of the M-Bots microbotic operations group and sets up a flash meeting to unveil the concept of the "O" for use by multiple industries. He also contacts Jason

Sanger, the head of design concepts at SpaceX, to suggest future applications for the miniaturized technology in the planning of SpaceX's upcoming Europa 7 project, never mentioning the source of the new product's name, "O," or the idea behind the processes leading to the invention of the concept.

Sanger warms to the idea, but reminds Sayre and the team that miniaturization can extend only so far towards the infinitely small. But he also conveys confidence that the scale Sayre presented seems doable for further investigation into the development of equipment necessary for the Europa 7 project as it approaches its 50th year of development. He acknowledges that neither he, nor any member of his team, had envisioned the use of miniaturization in the process of exploring the frozen moon of Jupiter. He also seems to understand the concept that once the microbots have learned a process, larger teams of robots could use their stored information to repeat the process, enabling full-scale replication in a fraction of the time it would have taken to build at actual size.

"What if something goes wrong in one of the prototypes?" asks Sanger. "Will we be stuck with a hundred defective replicas?"

"The way I see it is that the microbots create only two prototypes at the outset, which after testing are made ready for launch," says Sayre.

"One of the two is sent to examine the moon's surface, and if it succeeds, several more are replicated from the one retained. If the first prototype fails, the remaining one is modified and another duplicate is made from that one. Since all are miniaturized from concepts created with the intent to produce full-sized counterparts, the engineers who created the plans for the scaled-up version can make adjustments as necessary to the miniature one, or the microbots can fix the issue on any of the miniaturized copies, and then test it again as needed."

"Will the miniature be as effective as one that's full size?" asks Sanger.

"We can't know that yet...and it probably wouldn't be identical, but close... as long as we don't need to include a human or animal on board the spacecraft, it should be sufficient."

"How long would it take to make a prototype... of just "O"? asks Sanger.

"Perhaps three or four months," answers Sayre.

"At what cost?"

"I have no idea. But do you think the project is feasible?"

"Yes, I do. It's a different way of looking at space exploration, but it's been a theme in science fiction as far back as the early 1900s, and it became a recurring theme in the 1950s and 1960s in several films, including *Fantastic Voyage*. In each case humans were miniaturized, not robots. But, then again, we now make robots that are super small, and are able to communicate with them while they are in veins and other passages inside the human body."

"But it is unrealistic to think we could ever miniaturize humans. Your methodology allows us to miniaturize many of the functions of humans and incorporate them into smaller versions of themselves," answers Sayre.

He continues, "If we can have a camera operated by a microbot, and a vehicle piloted by that same type of robot, why would we even think of sending a human into the unknown until we find out if the prototype works as planned? In these cases, larger is not better. Smaller ships can maneuver more quickly than larger ships to avoid space debris, and they can be built and launched at a fraction of the cost of a vessel carrying human beings. The only thing we're not sure of is the size of the heat shield needed to protect the miniature craft during Earth's reentry, or in landing anyplace with a strong gravitational attraction. We would need more emphasis placed on parachutes to reduce the speed of descent to keep the miniature from burning up."

"Let's see what the Europa 7 team thinks," says Sanger. "I also want to run it by AI to get its opinion about the concept before we go any further."

"Sounds like a smart plan," answers Sayre with a smile, knowing his next call will be to Juniper Blakely, and already envisioning his friend's elation at the news.

Chapter Seven
Pittsburgh Bound

Based on John Sayre's encouraging response to the possibility of incorporating lifelike, moving figures into a large HO-scale train layout, Juniper sets to work outlining his concept for the presentation to the Pittsburgh Planning Commission. He is aware that he's rushing the process, since no prototype has been built and no costs have been projected.

Juniper has learned that the meeting venue on Friday has been changed from an online virtual gathering to an invitational televised broadcast at Sigmas, one of Pittsburgh's largest event centers. This reduces his available time for preparing visuals and creating a narrative for the unveiling of his plan – while it also ups the stakes, since it will be viewed by many more people. Juniper believes that he needs a "wow factor" in order to advance his project beyond a clever idea and into reality.

He plans to use his own railroad as a lead-in as well as an example of the quality of his workmanship. He also has decided to identify John Sayre's company, M-Bots, as the developer of the technology. Juniper realizes that he is taking a chance in mentioning Sayre, since Sayre has neither been notified that he will be mentioned in the presentation, nor has he made any claims to be able to produce even one prototype of the proposed figurines, let alone thousands.

Juniper understands that he has a history of jumping ahead on projects and promising untested concepts. He should know better, but his enthusiasm many times gets the better of him, so much so that he often fails to deliver on his promises. It's not that he doesn't know better. As a professional fact checker, he is often called on to investigate fraudulent claims, statements and agreements, many of which lead to prosecution. It is just that he truly believes that his concepts are sure hits that will work because he believes in them with every ounce of his being. Then, after his hopes turn to dust, he is devastated, blaming everyone he works with for their lack of vision before setting his sights on yet another concept, one that he believes in with even more intensity than the last.

With no functioning figurine yet created, Juniper reaches for ways of convincing the commission of his ability to produce them without misleadingly suggesting that they already exist. He also realizes that at least one person at the presentation will ask about developmental costs. Juniper knows this is unavoidable since Sayre alluded to the matter during their conversation. In response to that probability, Juniper makes up a number that sounds feasible, the first of many costs which he will conjure up from thin air.

Without stating his motives, Juniper again contacts Sayre and asks the engineer to share with him his sketches of "O" and of the simulation of a walking HO-gauge male. Sayre is hesitant, but ultimately consents and provides the visuals to Juniper via email. After receipt, Juniper redraws the sketch of "O" and adds copy, and although still not as far along as he would like to be in the process, Juniper is consumed by the fear that he has only one shot at this chance with Pittsburgh, and he's determined to make it the best he can within the time constraints.

Motivated by a sense of urgency, Juniper roughly learns and uses a photo and video editing program to simulate the walking of an elderly couple he's photographed from his layout, carrying bags at a railroad station. At first he thinks it would be a wise move to confess after the presentation that the video of the old couple is a simulation, but when the facsimile turns out better than expected, he decides to conclude his presentation with the couple walking towards the screen without a description.

Once he arrives at the event venue, Juniper is made aware that several groups have been invited to hear him speak, a detail not previously shared with him, as he had prepared for an online gathering. Either his contact forgot to tell Juniper, or enthusiasm for the project had widened and spread through internal media to many departments within the city.

Friday, 10:00 AM
The WBU Event Venue
Guest Speaker: Juniper Blakely
Topic: The Gateway to America

The morning is brisk as sunlight creates long shadows as early as 8:30. A light, post-breakfast event is planned at which will be served coffee, tea, and a variety of pastries. There are many familiar faces from the City Planning Commission, the Tourist Bureau, the Andy Warhol Museum, the Frick Art Museum, the Carnegie Museum of Art, and the Heinz History Center. Also in attendance are several members of the Greater Pittsburgh Chamber of Commerce, the Chamber of Commerce of Pittsburgh, the East Liberty Chamber of Commerce, and the African American Chamber of Commerce of Western Pennsylvania.

The invitation had sparked interest, as did its headline, "Pittsburgh's History in Miniature," and its sub-phrase, "Connecting America through Industry and the Imagination." The trifold-printed catalogue was copied in digital form for social media and includes the Steelmark logo at the center of a closeup map of the intersection of the Allegheny and the Monongahela Rivers as they join the Ohio River to become a gateway to the West. Pittsburgh was, and still is, an industrial city of unions and strikes, and a stronghold of a grass roots version of democracy.

Juniper arrives early and is met by technicians, council members and meeting planners who had traveled from the surrounding counties as far east as Clinton, Potter and Mifflin. He's surprised at the early turnout, but pleased by the number of representatives of small and large businesses, the arts, and the cultural elite who have apparently understood the potential of the concept of their history being told through model railroading.

Of course the crowd expects more, hoping to be further seduced by Juniper's vision of Pittsburgh as the center of progress in America. Though mentioned in the collateral brochure accompanying the invitation, the vastness of the scheme unveiled is merely an overture to the wonders yet to be revealed.

"How did they get so many to come?"wonders Juniper as he mentally reviews the timeline from his first contact until today. "It really should have taken much longer to arrange."

By 10:00 AM the chatter is loud and anticipatory as the mayor of Pittsburgh, Charles Nelson Taft, walks to a podium emblazoned with the city seal and attempts to quiet a crowd that exceeds the seating capacity of the auditorium.

"Ladies and gentlemen, please be quiet. I know we are all excited to hear of the new project proposed for our great city of Pittsburgh by the planning commission and Juniper Blakely, a young man with a dream that might prove to boost our economy, attract business, provide meaningful jobs for many, and lead us to prominence as a major destination point for tourism in the United States.

"Mr. Blakely has a passion for the past while living very much in the present, has been employed as a fact checker for the venerable firm of Enstro Technologies for the past 11 years, and brings to us an idea intended to celebrate our history while exhibiting our dominance in the use of cutting edge technology.

"I know you want to hear Mr. Blakely speak, and not me, so without further ado, I present Mr. Juniper Blakely."

Juniper walks across to the podium from a seat at stage left, places his notes down and adjusts his mic.

"Good morning, Pittsburgh!" (some cheers and applause)

"Unless you are fans of model railroading, most of you probably don't know me or recognize my name. My job as a fact checker is fairly low-profile, and my credentials are of little importance, except that I have a passion for history, a nostalgic affinity for our country's periods of growth, and a love of what seems to now be the craft of creating miniature worlds. That being said, I am not an historian, I have no degree in city planning or economics, and I have modest skills in the craft of model making in comparison to many of my colleagues.

"I am also not a modeling purist, in that I view technology as a way of enhancing the experience one gets from operating equipment from the past, as well as the understanding people gain while watching a farm or factory in operation, or the actions of a welder or a roofer at work, or the joy of children dropping into a stream from a rope swing tied to a tree limb overhanging a pond.

"I'm here today to present my vision for a model world with Pittsburgh at its center. In that world, America reaches eastward toward Philadelphia, northwesterly to Chicago and southwesterly to Ohio and the mid-west. Mine is a miniature story of the industrialization of America beginning with the Pennsylvania Railroad Company's railroad that in 1846 connected Pittsburgh to Harrisburg. By 1882, the Pennsylvania Railroad had become the largest transportation enterprise and the largest corporation in the world.

"Over the years it merged or acquired 800 other lines and companies, eventually merging with the New York Central Railroad.

"In short, my vision is to tell that story, at 1:87 scale, without commentary, but rather by observation of the simple acts of farming and manufacturing, the building of the Pennsylvania Turnpike, and the creation of the high speed lines that today connect the cities of Pittsburgh and Philadelphia by a trip lasting only 45 minutes.

"The world I envision will include the development of the fast food industry, the effects on communities during the Great Depression, and the birth and decline of drive-in movies, hot shops, juke boxes, 45 rpm records, amusement parks, prom queens and the fight for gay and women's rights.

"This project will start small, with the building of a miniature version of the horseshoe curve near Altoona, a feat that reduced the travel time by rail between Pittsburgh and Philadelphia from four days to fifteen hours. The next stage will be to compress the expanse between Altoona and Pittsburgh, and then start construction of the latter city as it began to grow. Historical landmarks will include the H.J. Heinz Company, Alcoa, Bayer and Pittsburgh Plate Glass. From there the layout will expand into the twentieth century, as the rail lines made their way eastward and turned toward the northwest, landing in Chicago. Tunnels will divide the passage of time, with an 1884 engine disappearing on the eastern slope of a mountain and reappearing as a diesel six decades later on the western slope. (At this point Juniper provides, as an example, a visualization on the screen behind him of a steam engine entering a tunnel, the screen turning dark, and then a more modern engine exiting through the time warp tunnel into a later era.)

"Today, train layouts contain more activity than just railcars pulled along tracks by engines. Technology has permitted us to watch lifelike cars driving along unblemished streets, stopping for lights, turning corners, and accelerating and braking realistically. Here is an example of a drive-in movie theater created by a fellow railroad enthusiast who based his layout on the 1950s. The cars shown are programmed to drive into their viewing slots shortly before the movie *Casablanca* begins on the screen. After all cars are situated, the movie continues for a few minutes before the ending credits appear and the cars leave their slots.

"Some of you in the audience may know of large layouts similar to those I've planned. Hundred are now located in all parts of the world, with each covering acres of ground. Some wander through various countries on their journeys, others randomly pass through time warps to new decades. Many show their cities darkening quickly to night with lights inside and outside homes and businesses turning on, and then reversing the process as dawn approaches. Many layouts also feature cars that drive down highways and travel through small towns. But none — let me repeat — NONE have people walking, running or interacting.

"Thanks to John Sayre, a model railroad enthusiast and executive director of M-Bots, 'Pittsburgh in Miniature' will be the first layout anywhere to incorporate HO-gauge people capable of realistic movement. (Juniper shows Sayre's reworked artwork of an 'O' with a human figure half that size positioned next to it.)

"So as not to get too technical, John's firm has already created microbots that can build even smaller robots. Because the robot he is building is the size of an O-gauge human – approximately 2 inches high, he is currently working on a way to have similar robots create other realistic robots one-half their size, or 1 inch high, but with legs and arms that move, hips that rotate and bend, and heads that turn, all of which will operate along an electromagnetic track that lies beneath the dirt, grass or roadbed. These remarkable robots will add a dimension of life to our layout never reached before.

"All of the details have not yet been worked out, and we are a long way from even beginning the first steps required by city officials. But with your support and approval, Pittsburgh can be a model for other projects of its kind, and create financial opportunities for a workforce with talents and abilities in a wide variety of skill sets. Jobs will include software design, layout design, carpentry, model making, painting, landscaping, weathering, assembly, and repair and maintenance, with future openings suitable for all age groups. The project will take ten years to complete, but could be open to the public in five. New segments created over time will entice return visitors, while targeted promotional efforts will draw new visitors from all over the world to visit the city to shop, eat, and be entertained, thus creating millions of dollars of revenue for the greater Pittsburgh area.

"I am appreciative to the Pittsburgh Planning Commission for inviting me here to present my concept, and will be taking 15 minutes of questions before leaving. Thank you for your support. I am hopeful that we can travel this road together. Now those of you with questions may raise your hands."

While awaiting the first question, Juniper's video mock-up of the elderly HO-gauge people walking to the tracks from the station appears on the screen, fading to black and then looping as a train pulls into the station from the right and slows to a stop.

Chapter Eight
It's a Wonderful Life

Juniper can't wait to inform Leonder about the positive response by the city of Pittsburgh to his model railway proposal. He contacts her shortly after leaving the auditorium with details of the meeting.

"It's overwhelming how receptive they all were, and how many leaders of different segments of government and industry attended... members of the City Council, tourism board, and the chambers of commerce from the city and surrounding communities. It went better than I ever expected and the response to my ideas was upbeat, and in tune with the scope and vision I've had all along for the project."

Leonder's pleased, but cautious in her response, since Juniper's enthusiasm often exceeds the realities encountered, as he sometimes neglects to consider obstacles that might hamper his progress and dampen his spirits.

"When will you be home?" she asks, and adds, "Please try not to set your hopes too high. Your project is wonderful, but also extraordinarily large... far more complex than anything you've ever attempted."

Juniper is familiar with Leonder's *Debbie Downer* attitude, and shrugs off any hidden message she means to impart.

"I'm taking a shuttle home in the morning, Leonder," he answers. "I wish you could see things from my perspective instead of always looking at the downside of what I'm trying to create."

"I'm very proud of you," offers Leonder. "But sometimes you bite off more than you can chew."

The following day, shortly after his return home, Juniper's wristband signals a caller. It's John Sayre, and Juniper responds to the contact eagerly.

"Hi, John, good to hear from you. I was about to call you..."

Sayre interrupts, "I can't believe you mentioned my name and that of my company in your presentation yesterday, Juniper! It was all over the news."

Confused, Juniper doesn't know how to react. "I thought you would be pleased..."

"My insights were for your ears only, Juniper. I can't believe you used me and M-Bots to add credibility to your plan without asking my permission. It was totally inappropriate, and I am appalled by your blatant inconsiderateness."

"I'm sorry!" says Juniper, at a loss for more words.

"I'd have thought you would have known better than to introduce to the world a concept neither you nor I have fully developed. I've been getting calls since the news broke yesterday. Many were from M-Bots board members, who asked why I hadn't alerted them about the project. Other contacts were from the engineers who work for me, asking me questions about the capabilities we currently have to produce such a line of products, and why we are entering a consumer market."

"I didn't think...," says Juniper.

"Obviously, Juniper. Asking my opinion is one thing, but broadcasting it as 'fact' is another. You, of all people, should understand that. Your job is scoping out facts and not in spreading rumors based on unsanctioned and untested opinions. Though I may have said that we might be able to produce a product, that doesn't mean the product is ready for release. You know better than that."

"I'm truly sorry, John. I jumped the gun on this, and I can see now that I let my enthusiasm get the better of me."

"I'm telling you right now that my team is drafting a release to the press negating M-Bots' connection with you and your idea. It will state that the company is not developing, nor does it intend to develop, miniature people for train layouts, doll houses, or displays of any kind. M-Bots is a technology-based company exclusively dedicated to the miniaturization of robots for the medical, aerospace and scientific fields.

"I needn't tell you this, but after your performance, M-Bots stock plunged 18%. Why? Because instead of being a leader in microtechnology, we look like we're a competitor of Mattel, Hasbro, or Fisher-Price."

After this comment, Sayre abruptly terminates contact with Juniper.

The effects of Sayre's rebukes hit Juniper on many levels. Only as Sayre provided a detailed description of the problem did Juniper begin to realize how inappropriate he had been in revealing details of his conversation with Sayre. While listening to his friend, he was able to clearly understand what he had done, as if hearing it from afar, and realized immediately how far out of

Leonder,

line he had stepped when publicly announcing his personal communication with Sayre.

And now, because of his stupidity, Sayre was going to destroy any chance of Juniper maintaining the credibility that he had established with the planning commission, or any of the other organizations that might have considered him for this once-in-a-lifetime opportunity.

Leonder, on hearing about the stunt, is shocked by her husband's lack of propriety. "You know that this might seriously injure your career, Juniper. My God, you are a *fact checker*, and you can't even control or convey truthfully your own facts!"

There was little Juniper could do to correct the situation. He had promised more than he could deliver in full view of the greater Pittsburgh community. He had alienated his friend. And he had placed himself in jeopardy of being looked on as a fool by any municipality that might have considered supporting his plan. Beyond that, as Leonder reminded him, his impropriety could cost him his job.

After begging Leonder's forgiveness, he contacts his boss and takes ownership of his mistake, apologizing profusely for any embarrassment his actions might have caused his department, as well as the company in general. Juniper's boss has long known of Juniper's passion for model railroading and, after listening patiently to his plea, he responds compassionately to the confession.

"We all make mistakes, Juniper," says his boss. "This is of minor importance to the company, and I doubt that it will raise any eyebrows among the higher-ups. My question to you is, 'Are you dissatisfied with your job here?'"

Juniper tries to be as truthful as he can be in giving his answer. "No. I like my job, and it's mostly interesting work, but you know my love of model railroading. I should know by now to be more careful than to let my passion cloud my judgment."

"If the opportunity ever comes for you to fulfill your passion, please let me know. My passion is the piano, and although I am only moderately talented, I would give anything to be able to support my family by playing music. If you ever succeed in fulfilling your dream, just make sure I have enough time to find a replacement. You're a good worker, Juniper, and a good man. I respect you for letting me know of your error.

"And remember, Juniper, only computers are perfect."

Comforted somewhat by his boss's response, Juniper retreats to his train layout for solace. Not in the mood to begin a new task, he cleans lengths of track while listening to the score from the 1936 movie *The Informer*. He tries to put his actions behind him but is reminded of his mission to animate figures by the inert molded figures populating his layout, caught in time and mid-task since they lack the ability to hoist barrels, sweep floors, walk dogs or enter stores with their children.

Nearly an hour into his mind-numbing chore, Juniper's wristband sounds. He checks the name and number and sees that it's from a Faye Gunther, a person he doesn't know and from an area code he doesn't recognize: 724, one of two listings he finds for the county of Indiana, Pennsylvania.

"Hello?" he answers hesitantly.

"Is this Juniper Blakely?"

"Yes, it is. May I ask who's calling, and how I may help you?" Juniper's index finger is poised for deletion, as he assumes that the contact is a computer.

"Hello, Mr. Blakely. I'm Faye Gunther, and I attended your presentation yesterday."

Still doubtful that the contact is human, Juniper asks. "And what is the reason for your call?"

"I'm the Executive Director of the Indiana County Tourist Bureau here in Pennsylvania, and I was impressed with your presentation yesterday. I am well aware that you were pitching a large-scale project to the Pittsburgh Planning Commission, but many of the county tourism bureaus were invited to attend. I brought along Nancy Boyle, the Director of the Jimmy Stewart Museum and Foundation, who was impressed as well."

"Jimmy Stewart, the actor?" questions Juniper.

"Yep, that's the one. He was born and raised in Indiana," answers Faye.

"I'm a big fan of his films...*Vertigo*...*The Man Who Knew Too Much*...*Mr. Smith Goes to Washington*..."

"Well, that's good to hear. Many don't know of him since he passed away more than 60 years ago."

"Yes, but *It's a Wonderful Life* still remains one of the five all-time favorite Christmas movies."

"Actually, it's risen recently back to number one," states Faye. "It has returned from third place to first place in two years after sinking to 11th in 2032."

"Nostalgic movies have made a comeback," answers Juniper. "A friend of mine has a copy of *It's a Wonderful life* on two reels. My wife Leonder and I watch it with him, his wife and friends every year."

"Then you might be interested in our concept."

There's a pause while Juniper contemplates his recent setback.

"Before you begin, I have to admit I made a big mistake yesterday at the meeting."

"You did?" answers Faye.

"Yes, it's quite embarrassing. I made a claim that was in error."

"What was that?" asks Faye.

"I discovered today that I won't be able to provide the animated figures of which I spoke in my presentation. The company I hoped to work with has announced that they aren't going to be manufacturing them for me."

"Oh, my!" says Faye.

"I made a false claim," admits Juniper.

"Well, can you do everything else you proposed?"

"As far as I know, I can. What do you have in mind?"

"Do you even know where Indiana, Pennsylvania, is?" asks Faye.

"No clue," says Juniper.

"Our town and county are east of Pittsburgh and besides being home to Indiana University of Pennsylvania, our most notable attraction is Jimmy Stewart and the museum named after him. We used to be the Christmas Tree Capital of Pennsylvania, but our production went way down in the 2040s when a blight struck our trees.

"Jimmy's last role was as an old man in *The Green Horizon*, and then he was the voice of Wylie Burp in *An American Tail: Fievel Goes West* in 1991. He died in 1997, and over the years the Museum and Indiana have been trying to breath new life into his legacy by positioning him as an historical figure and a person of great character, as opposed to being merely a famous actor.

"The truth of the matter is that for many years it was a struggle keeping the doors open, but in the past ten years or so the Museum has seen a resurgence of interest in Stewart's films, as there has been a reawakening to the classic film genre in general."

"I can personally attest to that," answers Juniper. "There's definitely an interest within my group of friends. It's somewhat difficult to explain why, but I guess it's the longing for a return to the traditions of film making, rather than the reliance on technology."

"I believe you're correct in your assessment," answers Faye. "In the beginning of this century, they colorized many of the black and white classics, including *It's a Wonderful Life*, but the colorized versions never caught on. And several years ago they remade the film using avatars that looked and spoke just like the original actors in the film. It was a huge flop.

"Recent surveys show that people between the ages of 30 and 50 have developed a keen interest in nostalgia, and the trend continues to grow.

"Our problem is that museums are a difficult draw in these times," says Faye sadly. "We've tried adding technology, but there's not much we can do to enhance attendance and promote our products, except for *It's a Wonderful Life*. That's a film that keeps on pleasing and gaining new fans."

"I can understand that. It's quite a film."

"It is, but it's not enough of an attraction. So here's an idea that Nancy and I dreamed up, based on your presentation.

"In our concept, Bedford Falls, the fictional location of the film, merges with the borough, becoming a suburb of Indiana. People who visit our downtown expect Philadelphia Street to be similar to Bedford Falls, and in most ways it's not. We have traffic signals that speak in Jimmy's voice, and Jimmy's original family home still stands high above the town on Vinegar Hill, but otherwise we are just like any small college town in Pennsylvania or, for that matter, anywhere else in America.

"Our history goes something like this. The town of Indiana was built in the early 1800s on land donated by George Clymer, one of the signers of the Declaration of Independence. The Stewart family's history parallels the story of much of the county, and reaches back five generations from Jimmy. To many fans, Stewart represents the ideals and industriousness of his hardworking ancestors and they recognize him as the symbol of the American dream. His legacy is tied to the characters he played in his films, like the lawyer, Mr. Smith, the smooth talking Macaulay Connor from *The Philadelphia Story*, the pilot/hero Charles Lindbergh and, of course, George Bailey, the protagonist of *It's a Wonderful Life*.

"We envision our story the way Frank Capra, as an immigrant, may have imagined George Bailey's story when he wrote it," continues Faye. "Capra wasn't from Pennsylvania and wasn't a Presbyterian like Jimmy. He was a first generation Italian-American who drew inspiration from the birthplace and character of his star, Jimmy Stewart, and invented the community of Bedford Falls, a place of do-gooders and others with evil minds, of heroes and villains, and of hopes for the future in the face of a decaying past."

"I get it, but what's my role, if I choose to take on the task?" asks Juniper.

"Your role is to make people believe Indiana is Bedford Falls each time they visit here, and to encourage as many people as possible to visit our town and county for the historic and dramatic experience of just being part of the town as imagined in the 1940s: dining in restaurants, having sodas at a counter in the drug store or a drink at Martini's Bar, and living in an atmosphere of a world that's a better place — just because of the town being here."

"That's a tough assignment," says Juniper.

"It's not as grand a vision as the one which you had hoped to achieve," points out Faye. "And we don't need it reduced to 1:87th scale, and don't necessarily need the whole population to be animated."

"Grand enough, still," says Juniper. "So where I failed, I may now have the opportunity to succeed?"

"By imagining success, you already have," replies Faye. " Welcome home, George Bailey. Welcome home."

Chapter Nine
It's a Wonderful Life – Refrain

Before considering any working relationship with the county and borough of Indiana, Pennsylvania, Juniper knows that because of his indiscretion, he should contact the Pittsburgh City Planning Commission concerning the project under consideration. Despite Sayre's threats, no one has contacted him from the media or from any of the organizations connected to the greater Pittsburgh area, other than Faye Gunther from the Indiana County Tourist Bureau.

Though fearful of rebuke, Juniper schedules a virtual meeting with Regis Delsey of Pittsburgh's Planning Commission, along with the city's mayor, Charles Nelson Taft. Both men are present in the electronic meeting when Juniper joins in as the host. They cast their glances away from the screen when he begins to speak.

"Thank you for accepting my request for a chat," says Juniper. "I assume you have both heard about my miscommunication with John Sayre of M-Bots."

Both men shake their heads in bewilderment and look down at their hands.

Juniper begins, "I wanted to apologize, for the way..."

Taft interrupts before Juniper can finish his sentence. "You do realize that it was an embarrassment to us, don't you, Mr. Blakely?"

Juniper nods a "yes" and Mayor Taft continues, "We really liked your idea and we trusted you, and now all of us who supported your idea look like fools."

" I know...," starts Juniper.

"No, you don't know, and I am going to tell you that you needn't have promised so much. We were sold on the idea, but you kept on going, promising things you couldn't deliver, to the point of lying about the progress you have made on the 'novelty' of animated figurines you proposed without permission.

"One of our problems is that we like you and your idea, but an attraction as large as the one you proposed will be extremely costly, and we don't believe we can trust you to deliver all you say you can.

"So here is our proposal to you: we will offer you the job of consulting on and guiding the design of the project, but those of us in charge at the city level would like to work with a company better suited to our needs to build and market the attraction."

"You still want to work with me?" asks Juniper.

"Yes. But there will be limits set on costs and complexities, and the way our city's history is presented. You won't be calling the shots."

"Then you're taking the project away from me."

"No. We're going to pay you for your ideas, and you can offer constructive concepts that we may consider, or not consider, as the project progresses."

"I appreciate that," answers Juniper. "But who will I be working for?"

"We are considering Mr. Sayre's firm, M-Bots, for the job."

"But John told me that he didn't want to work on projects unrelated to science," snaps back Juniper.

"Well, that isn't what he told us, and he says he'd be delighted to work with you in creating a plan..."

"It's my plan!" exclaims Juniper. "It's my idea, not his."

"As I said, we will pay you well for your concept, and even give credit to you as an advisor."

Juniper burns hot within as he thinks of how Sayre chastised him for naming him and his company in his presentation. He grows more angry as he realizes that Sayre has stolen the project away from him. But he also knows that Leonder will be furious with him if he turns down a proposal without knowing how much they are offering.

"What's your price, Mr. Taft?"

"Since it's only an idea, we think that $600,000 is more than enough."

"I've already received a counteroffer for my concept," Juniper lies. "And it's from a nearby county."

"You choose to negotiate, Mr. Blakely?"

"No, I choose to build my own project. You were one of several cities I contacted about creating an attraction that would captivate and educate in a way unlike others have done, and you specifically asked me to hold off selecting any competitor prior to meeting with you. Many people heard me speak the other day, and heard you praise my concept. I also believed John Sayre to be a friend, and hopefully a contributor to my vision, but it appears I was wrong."

"Mr. Blakely... calm down. What you proposed was merely a concept, and we're asking to purchase the concept. If it's about the money...we'll see..."

"No, Mr. Taft. It's not about the money. It never was. But now it's the principle that's at stake, and since Pittsburgh doesn't deserve my project, I intend to build it elsewhere...perhaps somewhere nearby."

"You're bluffing, Blakely. We could see to it that you never take your idea anywhere after the stunt you pulled. But instead, we're offering you a job that pays nearly four times your current salary..."

A bit of a smile begins to curl on Juniper's lips as he watches the two men together on the screen, and the mayor lashing out.

Hmmm? I believe I've heard something like this somewhere before, he thinks, as he continues his discussion with Mr. Taft.

"What's your point, Mr. Taft?" Blakely states dramatically.

"My point is that we want to hire you."

"Hire me," smiles Juniper. "You started out at $600,000 and maybe you'll get to $800,000, Mr.... Potter."

"What are you talking about?" says Taft.

"The conversation between George Bailey and Henry Potter in the movie *It's a Wonderful Life,* when Mr. Potter, played by Lionel Barrymore, tries to hire Jimmy Stewart, as George Bailey, and take over the family's building and loan business."

"What's that got to do with our negotiations?"

"Everything, Mr. Taft."

Juniper, who just viewed *It's a Wonderful Life* again for the fourteenth or fifteenth time after his meeting with Faye and Nancy, continues speaking Frank Capra's speech, using nearly the identical words Jimmy Stewart speaks in the film.

"Doggone it!

"You sit around here and you spin your little webs...and you think the whole world revolves around you and your money.

"Well, it doesn't, Mr. Taft.

"In the whole vast configuration of things, I'd say you were nothing but a scurvy little spider.

"And it goes for you, too," concludes Juniper, as he ends his soliloquy by

clicking to Regis Delsey and pointing the cursor at him.

"What the hell are you talking about, Blakely?" demands the mayor.

"I've been approached by Indiana County to build a model railroad celebrating its history, the heritage of the Stewart family, and the story of *It's a Wonderful Life*, and I'm going to take their offer."

"What!!? They haven't any money to build such a thing."

"There you go again, Mr. Potter... Taft... whatever the f%#@ your name is. This is about more than money," says Juniper, on a roll. "And if you try to steal my concept, I'll sue you and the city.

"Everybody in the meeting room, as well as those who watched the news, heard all of the good words you said about me.

"And, concerning Sayre. You can't even bring him up, since he stole my idea from a conversation I recorded, dated and backed up. He confirmed his theft by meeting with you to take an end run around me. I needed his help, but he didn't come up with the idea. *I did.*

"So, Mr. Taft, you played ball with the wrong person, and now you can just watch as Indiana County gets what you can't have."

Chapter Ten
The New Model

Iᵗ's been two hours since Juniper abruptly ended his video meeting with Regis Delsey and Charles Nelson Taft. During that time he began to research Indiana's rail history from its origin as a supply connection for the Rochester and Pittsburgh Coal Company (R&P Coal), linking the vast coal resources of the county to the cities of Buffalo and Rochester, New York, as well as the more distant markets of New England and Canada. By the end of the 19th century, R&P Coal had obtained track rights for use of the Baltimore and Ohio (B&O) rails, which enabled the coal company to expand its operations to capitalize on the burgeoning iron and steel industries in Pittsburgh.

Although the Buffalo, Rochester and Pittsburgh Railway (BR&P) thrived on heavy freight, passengers were also transported, with service considered "second to none" along the spur line until 1955, at which time the B&O discontinued its service to Buffalo. The passenger station built in 1904 remained on Philadelphia Street in Indiana well into the 21st century, metamorphosing into a restaurant and then a tourism depot before being demolished in 2052. The rails continued to provide a shuttle service for coal between Homer City and the power plant north of downtown Indiana until 2044, by which time the plant had become obsolete and the rails ripped up to make room for a walking trail connecting Homer City and the northern edge of the county.

As Juniper envisions the layout of the model railroad, he realizes that he can accomplish several goals for the Stewart Museum and Indiana County and create a vast impact on the economy of the area for little expenditure. As he sees it, the project is far more manageable than what he proposed for a major city, like Pittsburgh, and could be built in the larger O-gauge scale. It also could include the Stewart family heritage within its story. But best of all, he has conceived of a plan to include in the layout the fictitious town of Bedford Falls, created by Frank Capra for *It's a Wonderful Life.*

Meanwhile, the messages have been piling up in Juniper's mailbox and messaging system from his contacts in Pittsburgh, few of which he has looked at or listened to, and none of which he has answered. He is well aware that Pittsburgh wants to use his concept, and knows that the mayor will contact him with an alternative offer, but Juniper now understands that his best attempt at succeeding on his own may be to work with Indiana and the Stewart Museum.

Leonder intimately knows this about her husband: he is focused, bullheaded, and impossible to dissuade once he has set a plan in motion.

Ignoring the messages, Juniper puts a call in to Faye Gunther. Surprisingly, she answers almost immediately, "Faye Gunther speaking."

"Hi, this is Juniper Blakely."

"I was just thinking about you," answers Faye. "Have you made any decision, or whatever it is you do, to take on a project like ours?"

"I have a question for you, Ms. Gunther," responds Juniper.

"Okay. And call me Faye, please."

"Faye, I've been thinking of taking a shuttle to Indiana to see your town, but you know the area, and it might help me to address a question I have before my arrival. I was wondering if you know what buildings, if any, are situated along the old rail line north of Fulton Run Road, where North 6th Street ends?"

"Let me think on that. I grew up in the borough and know it well, but I don't remember every street."

"On the aerial map it looks like there's still a lot of trees above Route 954, along with an old industrial complex."

"Yes! I have a childhood friend who grew up in that area. The rail trail goes up there now. There's a right of way and not much else."

"If there are four acres of land available, I have another idea that might interest you and Ms. Boyle."

"I can look into it. What about the model railroad idea?"

"It seems doable. Just thinking ahead to the future."

"It all sounds so exciting. Do you think that you'll be visiting us soon?"

"My job is my priority, and I can work from most anywhere, but I still need to devote enough time to it. Get me some information on the availability of land we discussed, and I will work out a time for us to meet in Indiana."

At the end of the call, Juniper goes through his recent contacts from Taft and Delsey. Taft has left a recorded message:

Juniper, this is Charles Nelson Taft speaking. It doesn't seem we got off to a good start in our negotiations. I have to say that I may have been a bit premature in my offer, and am sorry you took umbrage with our thinking on the project. This is a big investment for us, but a large opportunity, too.

I have spoken to Sayre, and explained the situation, and he says that he's fine with you being in charge, and will work with you to develop whatever technology is necessary to make your concept work. He said he was perhaps somewhat harsh with you, and that he will call you later. Please give me a call as quickly as possible, so we can review the next steps. We really look forward to working with you.

"Screw you, Taft," says Juniper to himself, as he smiles at his future prospects based on the interest in a much smaller project in Indiana. Having reviewed the resources needed for a project the size of Pittsburgh, he can see now that he may have bitten off more than he could chew for his first attempt. The Indiana project allows him room to grow into his idea at a feasible pace, and provides him with an international cadre of volunteers and suppliers with interests in model building, old films, and history and railroaders from which to chose in realizing his dream. Sayre has shown his colors, but he knows others in the robotics industry who would jump at the chance of creating the figures he needs to accomplish his goals. The Pittsburgh contact and connection proved that his concept was viable; the Indiana project would enable him to spread his wings a bit further and expand his range in the future.

With the *It's a Wonderful Life* connection somewhat secured, Juniper decides to confide in his film buff colleague and Erran Heights neighbor Falon Justy.

"Hey Falon," begins Juniper as he gets him online from his home office.

"Yo, Juniper! What's cooking?"

"I've been working on something special that you might enjoy being part of."

"Shoot."

"I won't go into all of it, but I've been kicking around an idea for a large-scale model railroad project, and I've been in touch with the tourism bureau of Indiana, Pennsylvania."

"The home of Jimmy Stewart," Falon answers back.

"Yes. The project includes a history of the rail line that connected the coal areas of Pennsylvania with Buffalo and Rochester, as well as a history of the Stewart family."

"Sounds intriguing. Go on."

"A woman by the name of Nancy Boyle was also in my meeting."

"The Director of the Stewart Museum?" asks Falon.

"Right again, Falon. Do you know everything about the film industry?"

"Not everything. Just a lot of trivia between the 1940s and the early 1970s."

"Well anyway, we got talking about the film *It's a Wonderful Life.*"

"The number one favorite Christmas movie....*still!*"

"Will you let me talk, please? My idea is to blend history and fantasy together by incorporating the town of Bedford Falls into the layout."

"Are you going to extend the railroad to Seneca Falls in New York State?"

"No, why?"

"That apparently was the town that was the inspiration for Frank Capra's vision of Bedford Falls. In fact, they had a museum up there, maybe still do, that celebrates the film."

"No, Falon. My idea is to situate the town of Bedford Falls just north of the Indiana borough, and place it along the rail line as it would have looked during the 1930s and 1940s."

"Sounds ambitious."

"I envision the layout taking up about an acre of ground somewhere within the borough and used as a tourist attraction. The layout would include the route of the spur line from Homer City, past the Philadelphia Street station, to the town of Bedford Falls, as seen in the movie, and continue past Bailey Park and Potter's Field to parts unknown."

"I read somewhere that Capra shot the film on the RKO movie ranch in Encino using part of the set from the 1931 film *Cimarron*," says Falon.

"Yep. There were 75 stores and buildings, a tree-lined parkway, a factory and residential area, and a 300-foot Main Street – all adapted from the *Cimarron* set," elaborates Juniper.

"A fun project..." says Falon. "With a lot of potential."

"So, would you like to fly out there with me? We can take a shuttle that will land at the Jimmy Stewart Airport. They have one of his own planes on exhibition there. Have you ever been to the Stewart Museum?"

"No, but I've heard about it. Sure! I'm up for a getaway."

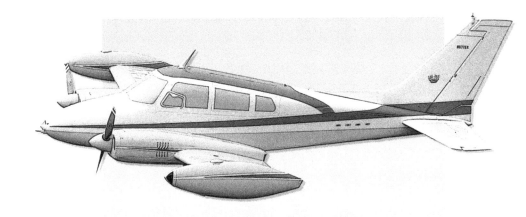

Chapter Eleven
Let's See What Happens

Hydroelectric air shuttle service has been available to and from most small airports since late 2037. Zero-emission transports can be hired by groups or individuals numbering up to 50, to fly non-stop for up to 3,000 miles. Top speed is 600 mph with the shuttles quiet and eco-friendly, and capable of landing and taking off from any airport or cleared field. Hydrogen fuel is stored in the wings to power as many as four turbines, with all ancillary electricity provided by solar cells bonded to the wings and fuselage of the aircraft.

Electromagnetic rail passenger pods located at the edges of the Crestoria community provide transportation to the Kern Valley Airport, every day on the hour from 6:00 AM to 9:00 PM. The system allows pre-scheduled residents to leave their homes at any hour and arrive at nearly any destination in the United States and parts of Canada and Mexico in less than five hours.

Juniper has plans to meet with Faye and Nancy at the Stewart Museum on the following Tuesday at 2:30, with an overnight stay for Falon and himself at the new Dobian Hotel on Philadelphia Street. They leave together from Juniper's pod at 7:30 AM for an 8:00 flight to Indiana, and are scheduled to arrive at the Jimmy Stewart Airport at 12:10 PM.

With only five days to prepare for the meeting, Juniper has been productive, if not obsessive, and realizes early on that he has aimed far too high and is moving way too fast in his thinking. He reminds himself that his priorities may not be other people's priorities, and that his approach may conflict with plans already set in motion. His proposal may be too costly, unrealistic in its scope, or depend on too many agreements of opinion to succeed.

By his nature, Juniper enjoys viewing the big picture, not bothered by restraints that can get in the way of his forward motion. He realizes that he rushed ahead with John Sayre, and though Sayre is also a "big picture" kind of guy, he doesn't have that go-for-it-all mentality that he himself has. In order to present a sense of control over the process, Juniper has laid out a semiannual timeline for a program to be developed over a five-year period, at the end of which the county and borough can expand the project, or choose to only maintain and manage what has already been developed.

Rather than overwhelming the women with an abundance of charts, graphs, videos and animations, he has printed out an outline of each stage, supported by simple graphics with Goldilocks variables that represent a range from "big plan" to "small plan" for each time period.

With only six others aboard the shuttle, the two men are able to spread out as Juniper guides Falon through his thinking process and objectives. Falon's role is to play devil's advocate to each of Juniper's ideas, responding with precision attacks aimed at weaknesses in Juniper's assumptions.

Juniper has brought along a portable printer for revisions, as well as background videos and material not included in the presentation.

"You know that each of the directors will have to share whatever they select with their boards," says Falon.

"I understand that," replies Juniper.

"They may be as enthusiastic as they can be, but a negative opinion from any member, for whatever reason, can be a death knell for your project," continues Falon.

"I totally am aware of that," answers Juniper.

"And you are way too excited to get started. These things take time."

"Pittsburgh didn't," responds Juniper.

"But you're not working for Pittsburgh, are you?" reminds Falon.

The time on the plane literally "flies," and before they know it the automated pilot announces their destination, with a landing in six minutes. The shuttle soon glides delicately to a stop.

Upon exiting, the men come face to face with Jimmy Stewart's 1961 Cessna 310F, restored more than 35 years ago, and maintained ever since in reverence for Stewart's love of flying and his record as a pilot in World War II, and as a tribute to the man who stood out as much for his deeds as for being a beloved actor.

A driverless vehicle is waiting for Juniper and Falon, and pulls out from its parking space to a safe zone near the runway. "Would you like to have a bite to eat before your appointment?" asks the car as the men settle into the rear seat. "It's 12:24 PM and your appointment is at 2:30. I can take you either to a restaurant near the museum, or directly to your hotel, whichever you prefer."

"Just take us to the hotel," answers Juniper. "They do have a restaurant there, don't they?"

"They do, but it isn't open for lunch," answers the car. "But there's a deli next to the museum that you can walk to after checking in. The wait time is reasonable, and I believe you will have enough time after check-in to have a sandwich, even if you spend a bit of time relaxing in your room."

The car whisks them down Philadelphia Street to the Dobian Hotel and stops at the entrance. The trunk pops open and the men's carry-on bags are lifted onto the ground near the curb.

"Enjoy your visit," says the car.

"Anything seem familiar about that voice?" says Juniper.

"Yep!" responds Falon. "Like everything else around here, it's Stewart's."

The Jimmy Stewart Museum is situated on the third and fourth floors of what was once the Community Center Building, which was completed in 1913 in the Spanish-Renaissance style. The town library moved into the first two stories in 1934 and the Stewart Museum moved into the third floor in 1995, finally occupying the top floor as well. Though plagued by years of financial difficulties, and the loss of interest because much of the audience for Stewart's movies had passed away, the museum struggled along primarily on the popularity of *It's a Wonderful Life* until the 2040s, when new generations of film buffs began to crave the movies of the 1930s, '40s and '50s.

In a 2044 issue of *Psychology Today*, an editorial by renowned psychologist Esther Blumfeld stated, "The world is changing much too quickly for all of us, and technology has advanced so fast that we have little understanding of it, or relationship with it. When watching many of today's films, the images are extraordinarily real, and there is no way of telling if the actors are animations or actual humans, the sets real or virtual, the music composed and performed by computers or by musicians, or the scripts created by AI or the imaginings of real people.

"From therapy sessions I've conducted, I find that most people don't trust anything or anyone anymore, their main complaint being that they feel manipulated by technology rather than in control of it. Classic films from earlier eras are a great escape from the ultra-realities of today. When

Fred Astaire danced, you knew that he had practiced over and over to perfect his every move. The Marx brothers made you laugh by performing the silliest of stunts, and Jimmy Stewart made you like him by being authentic. From what my clients tell me, there is nothing now that can be considered 'genuine.'"

Following lunch, Juniper and Falon walk across the street and are directed by signs to the Stewart Museum building and then to the elevator that takes them to the third floor exhibit hall. Faye and Nancy greet them at the door and provide a tour of the exhibitions of the stages of Stewart's career, beginning with his growing up in Indiana, and then his heritage, through letters, photos, posters, and costumes worn by the actor. One section of the museum is dedicated to *It's a Wonderful Life*, as is much of what is sold in the small store that adjoins the ticket booth.

After the tour, the group of four retreats to Nancy Boyle's office on the fourth floor to talk. Juniper is glad he has printouts of his plan, since there is barely enough room for a meeting there, let alone a video presentation.

"First of all," starts Juniper, "I am very pleased to have been invited to come to Indiana, and I look forward to seeing more of the town following our meeting. I have brought along a friend and movie buff, Falon Justy. He knows much more about classic films than I do, and has been most helpful in preparing my presentation.

"For me, the most remarkable and seductive reason for my interest is that you two sought me out, and had the vision to see the potential of my project without any actual knowledge of what I might do, or how I might approach it.

"Your vision placed a responsibility on me, which is something I have often been known to take too lightly.

"Before I agreed to a visit, I asked Faye about the availability of land to the north of the borough. That was not as pertinent, I discovered when entering your building, as the fact that the library is no longer located here."

Faye responds quickly to the implied question, "A new library was built at the other end of town in 2035 that is somewhat smaller than the space it occupied here. The new building is far more suitable for people than the space below us here. The new facility has more room for lectures and events, and less room for the display of books. Most of the books and periodicals are confined to bins and efficiently accessed by bots from an order desk. It now has four times as many computers for public use, a theater about the size of ours, and it uses drones to deliver books to shut-ins, hospitals and nursing home facilities on request."

"Then what are the first and second floors used for?" asks Juniper.

"More storage..and temporary county offices. They keep changing their minds about what will happen to the building in general."

"Are they thinking of demolishing it?" asks Falon.

"No, I don't believe that would serve any purpose," answers Nancy. "We value our history in this town, and have enough problems with the University taking over every empty space as it's grown. The business community has tried to limit development as much as possible to assure Indiana remains a small town."

"Could the museum take over the rest of the space?" asks Juniper.

"Theoretically it's possible," answers Faye. "But we don't really need that much room. The state and local governments, along with the community, funded the construction of the new facility since much of our building doesn't meet the newer codes. The museum, once funded primarily by the Stewart family, is now mostly funded by the tourism bureau, which gets its money from the hotel tax. Our budget makes a big dent in their budget. We do get some donations, and some financing from grants, as well as a little from our store. And every now and then we get support from a wealthy donor who loves classic films and wants to see us survive."

"What about the film industry?"

"Recently we've had some interest from film makers who want to use Jimmy's likeness in projects they're planning. Although the family set up a small trust to support us years ago, the newest generations can't financially provide us with the funds we need to grow. Photographs of Jimmy are mostly all in the public domain, and have been for some time, so the family leaves it up to us to decide what can and cannot be done when images are requested of Stewart. So far, we haven't had to release Jimmy to the world of actor avatars, but we may have to as time goes on. It benefits us to get Jimmy on the screen again, any way we can."

Juniper turns to Nancy and asks, "I believe you said that The Jimmy Stewart Museum is the largest attraction in Indiana?"

"Yes, besides the University. There's not much else in the county but some lovely parks and trails. We have some beautiful buildings in town, like the one that houses the historical society but, overall, we're just a small college town."

Juniper pauses, not knowing whether it's the right time to bring up his plan, or how much of it to bring up. Pittsburgh was willing to pay him more than $500,000 just for his concept, and Indiana County and the museum can barely support themselves.

Noticing that Juniper is wavering, Falon decides to jump into the conversation.

"You've asked Juniper to support your mission. As I see it, what you need to do is enhance the attraction of the county to outsiders by giving them reasons to visit more than once, and to return here for reasons other than visiting their children at college. To do this, you must enhance your offerings, and the most efficient way of doing that is by further developing the attractions you already have. The only ones I see are (a) Jimmy Stewart, (b) Jimmy Stewart's films, and (c) Jimmy Stewart as George Bailey in *It's a Wonderful Life*. End of story.

"Juniper pulled away from Pittsburgh's offer because he believes that your town and your history have more potential for success than their city does... or perhaps any of the cities to which he's proposed his concept.

"So, Juniper, don't be modest. These two courageous women are willing to evaluate your plan, work their butts off to find you the necessary funding, and assure you the support you need to guarantee a success for their community. Isn't that right, ladies?"

Faye and Nancy aren't exactly sure what Falon said, but they were mesmerized by the confidence he expressed in support of his colleague.

"As Director of Tourism for this county, it's my job to do whatever is possible to enhance the image of the county and expand the offerings for people who pass through," responds Faye. "We don't want to become a Disney World, but we do want to be thought of as something special, so we need to broaden our perspectives. That's why we approached you, Juniper. "

Nancy then adds, "We don't know what we want to do, let alone if we are able to do it, but we are willing to work with you, if you'll work with us. I feel confident about you and the project and excited by the thought of doing something challenging. And I believe that Faye feels the same way."

"Thank you, ladies! And thank you, Falon, for your vote of confidence in me."

At that point, Juniper hands the latest printouts to Faye and Nancy. "Based on the information you've just provided to me, there are already some changes to be made to my proposal. Let's see what we can get done, and then see what it will take to make this thing happen."

Chapter Twelve
The Return to a Tactile Reality

*A*ccording *to* trainorders.com, *there are 3.5 million model railroaders in the United States in 2060, nearly 2.5 times the number recorded 30 years earlier. Many tactile hobbies and crafts such as knitting, needlepoint, jewelry making and ceramics have also enjoyed an increase in participants as fewer people remain in the job market for more than 25 years, and the average lifespan has increased to 98 years in developed countries. 3-D printers,laser carving machines and wireless technologies have enabled model car, airplane and railroad enthusiasts to manufacture many of their own layout parts from plans provided online, making the creation of miniature buildings, vehicles, roadways trees, terrain and figures available to a wider market at extremely affordable prices.*

As pointed out by Jay Ligow, Director of the Western Pennsylvania Model Railroad Museum in Gibsonia, "Over the last 20 years, the average age of the model railroader has decreased from 72 years to 41 years. This was after years of declining museum membership and interest among younger people. In the last ten years we have tripled our membership, with many of the new members being in their teens or early twenties."

Ligow goes on to say, "Some of us are purists, and choose to make each building and setting from scratch, while a wider number enjoy 'kit bashing,' or modifying prefabricated kits to create personally designed buildings. Others take pleasure in the simple act of assembling, painting and aging buildings to evoke a particular era in their layouts. And many of our youngest members enjoy exploring the technology of the hobby, programming everything from the acceleration and braking of vehicles to the seemingly random scheduling of activities in the streets and train yards.

"Since the boom of electronic media in the early 21st century, virtual reality, video gaming, online gambling and relationship development have dominated the free time of people of most generations. But I believe that all trends are cyclical, and that the emptiness of the virtual world has lead people back to traditional activities as noted in the upswing in the tactile pastimes, including the arts, crafts and model building.

"There have been many changes in technology over the last 100 years, but the one thing that remains constant is that model makers have, for the most part, hearkened back to earlier times for their inspiration, when the pace of life was slower, outdoor activities were less structured, and people related to their neighbors by talking over the fence rather than by texting, having virtual meetings, or sharing stories, music, poems or gossip using electronic devices."

Instead of requesting an open-ended budget to build a grand attraction for a region, Juniper has simplified his focus and configured an affordable and workable plan that will serve to celebrate the history and heritage of Indiana County and Jimmy Stewart and his family, and expand on the allegorical story of the Capra film *It's a Wonderful Life*. His research has confirmed in his mind that his approach to a multi-stage project is advantageously timed, and that Indiana County is the optimal place to begin his journey into a career that will prove to be satisfying and matched to his personality and skill sets. This particular project blends his love of research with his passion for classic films, history and model railroading, and will rely on all of his abilities and interests in order achieve a successful outcome for the county, the museum and his own future.

Juniper is well aware that he needs the total support of the board of directors of both the tourism bureau and the Stewart Museum to realize his goals, as well as to assure a buy-in from the community. But mostly he is dependent on the hard work and imagination of hundreds of model railroad enthusiasts, robotics and technology experts, historians, film buffs and influential people in the film industry to make the project financially feasible.

After five weeks of planning, while balancing his job and family life, Juniper has fine-tuned his approach and is prepared to present his plan in person to the tourism bureau, the board of directors of the Stewart Museum and the community. He employed disciplines that he trusts will help him avoid the pitfalls experienced in Pittsburgh, one of which was to take all of the burden on himself, expecting little from those outside of his core group of enthusiastic supporters. He is well aware that the need for control has been both an aspect of his ego, and a new realization that the only way to get things done is to take on all of the responsibility for the success of his program.

The meeting is to be held in the old Rustic Lodge, a venue that has hosted events in the Indiana borough for more than 120 years. Although the lodge is a bit out of date, it remains the dominant location for weddings, funeral luncheons and parties within the borough, primarily due to strong community and familial traditions in the county. In recent years the technology in the lodge has been updated, but its facade and decor have miraculously remained much the same as they were a century ago.

The presentation is scheduled during a luncheon served on white clothed tables with cotton napkins, featuring warm rolls and butter, a chopped salad, and a choice of chicken, fish or vegan entrée. Juniper and Falon are seated at the table with the tourism director and her husband, the Stewart Museum's director and her husband, and George Elliot, the mayor of Indiana borough and his wife, Charlotte. No TV cameras are present, and there are no reporters. The guests attending are members of the Stewart Museum and tourism board of directors, members of the borough council and chamber of commerce, and concerned citizens who remain wary of projects that will result in too much change in the community.

The fact that Juniper and Falon are from California is of interest to all, as many believe California is defined by the glamour and glitz of Hollywood. They believe that most all individuals living in California are wealthy or prominent. All attendees have been briefed on the subject of Juniper's presentation, but not on the particulars of his concept.

As the coffee is being served, the Director of the Indiana Chamber of Commerce introduces Juniper, and provides a little personal background and a few words about his job and interests. Juniper steps to the podium amid mild applause.

"I am very happy to be here today to meet all of you and to learn more about your community. Faye and Nancy have been exceedingly open with me in expressing the concerns that some of you might have, including a too rapid increase in tourism, uses of land and resources that might impact taxes and the environment, and increased traffic within residential neighborhoods. In researching the county and the borough I have learned a lot about your history and your culture, and intend only to embrace your past, not exploit it.

"I assume that you want to know just where we'll start.

"Economically, it makes sense to work with what exists, and that will be to expand the Stewart Museum from its current occupancy on the third and fourth floors of 835 Philadelphia Street downward to the first and second floors formerly occupied by the library. Currently these floors are minimally occupied and together offer an expansion capability of nearly 9,600 square feet, more than doubling the museum's current size.

"You may have heard some rumblings about building a new facility, and ultimately the space will need to be larger, but for now the second floor will be satisfactory for the first stage of my plan, which is to create a model of "Bedford Falls," Frank Capra's fantasy home town for his 1946 film *It's a Wonderful Life.*"

Juniper asks that the lights be dimmed and the projector turned on. He uses a light wand as a pointer to highlight locations on a map of Bedford Falls that appears on the screen.

"Some will think of this as a standard O-gauge train layout, but at this stage in development I envision only two trains running on the same track – a passenger train and a freight train both leaving Homer City from the south, going past the Indiana station on Philadelphia Street, and on to Buffalo, New York. The main stop on our line will be the station where George Bailey's brother, Harry, returns home to Bedford Falls as a former star athlete in college. The pond where Harry falls through the ice as a child and is saved by his brother George is just north of the station, while Genesee Street, the main avenue and parkway of Bedford Falls, runs across the middle of the layout and is lined by more than 30 stores and buildings featured in the film. They include a hardware store, *The Sentinel* newspaper office, a grocery store, two cafés, a music shop, the Bijou Theatre, a meat market, and Gower's Drug Store, where George Bailey worked as a boy.

"Mary, George's future wife, grew up and lived until her marriage on Sycamore Street, shown here not far from the station, and Mary's house on Sycamore is the Old Granville Mansion that will later become the "drafty old house" owned by George and Mary. Bridge Street intersects Genesee near the courthouse and plays a pivotal role in the film in that it is the location where George wrecks his car after a few drinks at Martini's Bar and then heads for the toll bridge to end his life.

"The two housing developments, Potter's Field, shown here, and Bailey Park, over there on the other side of Genesee, are equidistant from the courthouse.

"And where is Indiana? At this stage of development, it is the larger town south of Bedford Falls, as shown here on an expanded map of the Indiana borough.

"Any questions so far?"

"I have one," says a council member. "As I see it, what you're proposing is a children's toy train layout....with only two trains...on a single track? That's not much of an attraction."

"It may seem that way," responds Juniper. " But here's how the layout becomes quite different. The action on the model will follow the action of the movie from beginning to end, with the cars, people and situations changing in time with the movie. The model is played out in the exact sequence as the film, and is choreographed to the original soundtrack.

"Take a look at this scene where George Bailey jumps off the bridge. The animated figure of George on the model will also jump into the water to drag Clarence, the guardian angel, to safety."

Juniper plays the scene on the screen.

"Another example is when George meets Mary at her house and Mary sings *Buffalo Girls* as she strolls with George. The movement of the figurines on the layout will duplicate the couple's movements on the screen.

"And take a look at this indoor scene when George and Henry Potter discuss George's future. Visitors will watch the shadows of the characters against the window shades of Potter's office while they converse in the movie."

"That's a lot of work," says the same council person. "It's also very complicated. Are you sure you can do this?"

"My concept is to add a new dimension to the story, giving it a sense of place. In our model, that place is located just north of the Indiana borough."

"But wasn't Seneca Falls, New York, the inspiration for the original story and the film?" asks one of the members of the tourism board.

"Possibly, but in reality Bedford Falls was a composite of every small town in America. Indiana is the real home of Jimmy Stewart. And Capra's inspiration for George Bailey came from here, not New York or Hollywood. What we'll be doing is adding a tangible component to the film. The experience is intended to evoke a memory in the viewer of the setting being a real place and not a constructed fantasy.

"And, by the way, the whole layout will be created in black and white, just like the film."

"Excuse me," says a tall thin man with bow tie at a table reserved for community members. "What can we expect to see happening in other areas of the layout as each scene in the movie is being duplicated?"

"Good question," says Juniper. "The ongoing action pauses, or slows down, during the enactment of the scenes. Cars still drive by, and people still walk down streets and go about their business. If it's snowing, it continues to snow. If the moon is out, it stays lit. The objective is to follow the storyline while experiencing the action...as plays often do. Actors can continue to speak to each other very quietly as long as they don't interrupt the featured dialogue. I also plan to gently spotlight and direct focus to each scene on the layout while it is played on the screen."

"How much will this thing cost..." asks a heavyset man at another community table. "How can we know that whatever you plan will be worth the money...and who is going to pay for it?"

"Since I began thinking of a project like this on a grand scale, I have learned a lot. I know that all of what I hope to do is possible, to tell this part of the story. If you embrace my proposal, my wife Leonder and I will lease our pod in Crestoria and move here to supervise the project. I will continue working for the company I currently work for remotely, but will be reducing my hours to devote as much time as I can to the planning and building of the Bedford Falls pilot program.

"Falon Justy, the fellow sitting next to Faye, has contracted with a documentary production crew to follow the project as it develops. Before we left our hotel late this afternoon, he informed me that he has found the financing to support the making of the film.

"This initial stage will take two years to complete. I have been in touch with the Western Pennsylvania Model Railroad Museum in Gibsonia, and many of its model maker members have agreed to donate their time to construct the town and surrounding buildings for the cost of the materials. I have also patched up a relationship with a friend of mine, John Sayre, the CEO of M-Bots, a robotics firm, who will be donating his and his company's time to create a prototype of a human figurine to be used in multiple forms to allow the characters to move realistically.

"The film *It's a Wonderful Life* is once again in the public domain, as is the musical score. The Pittsburgh Symphony Orchestra has agreed to adapt Dimitri Tiomkin's original score to fit the layout's multimedia format. This includes more than 30 minutes of music from the original score that was left out of the film, and some new segues adapted from the theme music. If all works are approved, the orchestra plans to issue a recording of the adaptation after the project is completed.

"We all know that this is a speculative project," Juniper emphasizes. "But one that Faye, Nancy and I believe will shine a new light on Indiana, and rekindle an interest in the borough and the legacy of Jimmy Stewart.

At this point, I envision this to be the first segment of a larger project. Faye will begin promoting the concept to the press as soon as we get started, and Nancy plans to use local contractors to prepare the second floor to meet the needs of the layout. Knowlton & Giday, the architecture firm we plan to partner with for the design of the layout, is renowned for its work on major miniature worlds, including *The Building of the Brooklyn Bridge* in New York City, *The Age of Dickens* in London, and *The Taiping Rebellion* in Shanghai. Their work does not come cheap, but they are familiar with the technology of integrating film with the physical layouts.

"Projected costs are between $2.5 and $3 million, with most of the money coming from an increase in the hotel tax throughout the county. Indiana University of Pennsylvania has already agreed to contribute $.5 million to support the program.

From a rear table in the lodge, a woman raises her hand to grab Juniper's attention. "Excuse me," she says after Juniper acknowledges her. "You mentioned that this is only the first part of the project. What do you see coming after that?"

"I see the model expanding beyond Bedford Falls, and occupying a much larger space to celebrate the region, though not the entire history of Indiana County. It will focus on the county during the industrial age and will concentrate on the coal industry and how the railroad was used to transport coal and minerals to New York, New England and Canada. There are many directions we can choose going forward. I believe the University sees this as an educational opportunity as well as an attraction, one that will elevate its status and increase enrollment.

"Personally, I have other ideas, but they are premature at this point. Hopefully we will be able to work together on expanding the scope of the Stewart Museum and helping to increase the number of visitors looking to Indiana as a destination point. Once the impact on the community is evaluated, you may decide to cautiously proceed further."

Another hand goes up and is acknowledged by Juniper. "Why are you willing to take this project on at this point in time?"

"I have a passion for model railroads, and love classic movies. I also identify with George Bailey from *It's a Wonderful Life*. He dreamed big and had to compromise his dreams before realizing he already had everything he wanted in life. I believe the movie ends too soon and think that George Bailey should have built on his vision. Though never becoming the architect he hoped to be, he might have risen to great heights based on his willingness to fight for that in which he believed.

"If the community takes on this project, I will have a chance to live and work in Jimmy Stewart's hometown and build a new version of Bedford Falls. Like Clarence the angel, who puts George Bailey's life into perspective, I still have a long way to go to earn my wings."

Chapter Thirteen
Harry Bailey Returns – The Prototype

*T*he Bedford Falls station is used only once in the film It's a Wonderful Life, *but is seminal in describing the joy and sorrow that George Bailey experiences when welcoming his brother back to Bedford Falls after four years away, meeting his new wife, Ruth, and learning that Harry isn't intending to return permanently to Bedford Falls. Instead, after a short visit, his plans are to continue north to Buffalo, New York, to work as a research technologist for his father-in-law's glass business.*

The scene depicted in Juniper's test model opens with a starlit sky projected onto a ceiling. Two stars are conversing, reflecting on George Bailey's announcement to his staff at the building and loan that Uncle Billy would be taking over for him, now that he has finally gotten his chance to go to college.

Star No. 1: "I know, I know, he didn't go."

Star No. 2: "That's right. Not only that, but he gave his school money to his brother Harry, and sent him to college. Harry became a football star and made second team all-American."

Star No. 1: "Yeah, but what happened to George?"

Star No. 2: "George got four years older, waiting for Harry to come back."

The rising frequency of the engine's whistle and the squeal of the steel wheels on the rails announces the arrival of the train delivering Harry and his bride to Bedford Falls. The sky brightens and the stars disappear as a soft white beam focuses on George Bailey telling Uncle Billy his plans for the future while pointing out places in brochures that he hopes to travel to and make a name for himself now that his brother is home from school and can take over the family business. Then George hears of Harry's marriage, and his brother's move to Buffalo for a job with Ruth's father, and his own dreams are once again destroyed. But George, being the man he is, remains upbeat and pleased for his brother. He even shares popcorn with Ruth as she tells him what a wonderful researcher Harry is.

The scene closes and day once more turns to night with the moon casting deep shadows on the Bailey family home. A party is taking place inside with banners and balloons embellishing the celebration of Harry's return. Mrs. Bailey joins her son George on the porch, amidst laughter, drinking, music and dancing by friends, family and neighbors. George and his mother speak warmly to one another and Mrs. Bailey urges George to visit Mary, who's back from school. George has somehow heard that Mary is dating another man and stubbornly marches off in the opposite direction of Mary's house to Genesee Street, the main boulevard of Bedford Falls.

George's stroll down the parkway is illuminated by street lamps that turn on ahead of him, choreographed to the song Avalon *playing on the Victrola in George's mother's house. He attracts the attention of Vi, a flirty girl, who abandons two male companions to chat up George, but George's idea of a good time and hers don't match, and the scene ends with George reversing his journey towards Mary's house, and tapping a stick he's found along the way on fence pickets, posts and mailboxes, innocently alerting the young woman of his presence.*

———

Though Juniper has not yet been given final approval by any organization in Indiana County to begin working on the *It's a Wonderful Life* railroad project, he proceeds in a way most who know him would expect of him — beginning *without* an agreement. Juniper is well aware of the pitfalls of diving head first into a concept without protecting himself by contracts and following processes and protocols.

He has already contracted with the architect Ezra Knowlton concerning the design plans for the station as well as the Bedford Falls schematic needed for construction.

He also has made amends with John Sayres, who he knows is as passionate about a project of this kind as he is.

"John. Juniper here," he speaks into his wristband with no emotion. "Here's where I am with the Indiana project. I have a snippet of action framed out and I need some microbots. Despite what you might admit, I know you've been working on this, so just tell me how long before I can get to see an O-scale operational figurine."

"Well, hello to you too, Juniper," answers Sayre. "Are we still enemies, or are we working together?"

"I thought that we were partners back in Pittsburgh."

"Okay. Are we done with the past, Juniper?"

"I hope so."

Realizing that Juniper has correctly assessed his motivation, Sayre begins with, "Here's what we've done to date. I have a prototype of an O-scale adult male and one of a female figure, both programmed to walk, run, sit, and move realistically in most directions and assume most positions. The composition of each form is generic, and adaptable. We have sheathed each with artificial skin that flexes, bends and shrinks back after every movement. The height, weight and body type of each figure can be adjusted to accommodate any size or age of individual.

"Children and animals have not yet been created, but we are working on them. The main stumbling block I see moving forward is the costuming,

80

which will require specialized microbots to stitch and assemble fabrics into clothing from full-size patterns. We still need other microbots to paint the faces and dress the figures. I've tried to decorate the prototypes myself, without much success. We must also address the need for more precise modeling of hair and makeup. The hair must not appear molded. It must flow.

"We've also created a selection of hands and feet positioned for special uses, such as holding a cigarette, riding a bicycle, carrying a briefcase, or wearing sandals."

"It sounds like you're making progress," says Juniper. "When may I see the prototype?"

"I'll send you a link to a video we've put together. It's impressive and will provide the complete range of capabilities."

"Thanks, John. I'll review it and get back to you. But here is what I will need very quickly for the prototype layout: I need George Bailey and Uncle Billy, men of different ages, size and body type. George in a gray suit and hat and Billy in white. I also need Harry and Ruth Bailey, four generic male porters - two black and two white, Bailey's mother dressed as in the movie, six generic women, Vi, and six men, with appropriate hats and hairstyles."

"How are you suited for cars?"

"I need a variety of static black '30s sedans, roadsters, coupes and a phaeton, plus an operational white coupe and black roadster. Overall, I will need several of each, especially static ones. And throw in a few gray cars. For this part of the project, as well as all others, everything is in grayscale."

"I think I can handle that," answers Sayre. "I hate to bring this up, but how and when do I get paid?"

"Money is being raised, but I have to show them something tangible before I can expect payment for anything."

"That means that you're working for free?"

"Yes."

"And you turned down $600,000 for the concept and for overseeing a project for Pittsburgh?"

"That's my business, John. Not yours," answers Juniper. "Regarding your part of the project, you will be paid $50,000 for the animated figures we need at the moment. I know that's less than what you think you deserve, but it's what the project can afford."

"What about the rest of the characters? You will need hundreds."

"Possibly thousands," answers Juniper. "But once you have your manufacturing facility up and running, you'll make millions. You and I both know that."

"And when do you need the characters – costumed, I am sure?" says Sayre.

"Yes, costumed. A month from now."

"One month! That's all the time I've got?"

"I know you can do it. I also know you've also been working on the microbots who will do the stitching and decoration."

"You don't know that," says Sayre.

"Come on, John. You and I both are like dogs on bones. The only difference is that I'm willing to put everything on the line, and you're not."

Sayre remains silent.

"I want this prototype ready for an unveiling at the Stewart Museum for Christmas of this year. That gives me five months to work on it, and I need the characters ahead of time to make sure that they do everything you promise they are capable of doing, and to be assured that the programming works."

"But I'll need at least six months for what you're asking."

"Time's a-wastin'. No napping!" says Juniper. "Just think of me as Henry Potter. I understand what you really want more than you do."

Summer Winter

∿ Bladder ∿

Chapter Fourteen
Technically Speaking

Using email and social media, Juniper reaches out to the community of model making members of the Western Pennsylvania Model Railroad Museum. Shortly thereafter, hundreds of photos and videos arrive in his inbox presenting a wide range of techniques for the construction of buildings, bridges, neighborhoods, railway cars,and miniature accessories from submitters, all hoping to be selected to assist with Juniper's project. Many of those responders passed on Juniper's request to other model railroaders who are also classic film buffs and who have experience in creating themed model railroads inspired by films of the 1930s and '40s.

Juniper has provided architects Knowlton & Gidday with a list of design priorities, the first being the completion of plans for the Bedford Falls train station, and the next being the development of the schematic drawings of the rows of buildings that will line both sides of the parkway on Genesee Street. To complete his prototype, he will also need detailed plans of George Bailey's mother's home on New England Street and Mary's parents' home on Sycamore.

Knowlton and his staff of architects are guided by stills from the film *It's a Wonderful Life* depicting the facades of homes and businesses, matching them with period photos of buildings in similar styles that still exist in towns across America. Although the buildings shown in the movie are stage fronts with partial or no interiors or side or rear walls, the layout calls for complete structures. Most will need illumination and some, like the Bailey home and Gower's Drug Store, will require the interiors to be partially visible through windows and doorways.

The map of the town, a joint effort by Knowlton's team and Juniper, is essential to the plotting of the action on the model as it synchronizes with the film. A walk or car ride from one location to another will lead the viewer through the journey, rather than the action being edited into segments as it appears in the film. This continuity will define some scenes, such as George Bailey's car ride from the bar to the toll bridge as he contemplates suicide.

After selecting the craftsmen needed for the project, Juniper sends out a list of general guidelines along with a site plan and photo reference for each assigned structure, a list of specifications and instructions for its packaging and a designated delivery date for each structure. Each participant must submit a progress report along with a video on specified dates. Meanwhile, local participants are placed in charge of creating landscapes for the buildings and other on-site tasks including terrain, street and sidewalk construction, and overall technical development.

Juniper arranges to leave his home in Crestoria to manage the construction project from the second floor of the museum. Leonder will eventually join him, as the couple plans to rent out their pod for an indefinite period of time through the first phases of construction. The borough has provided temporary living quarters on the first floor of the museum building until the couple can find a more permanent residence within the community.

Since the storyline of *It's a Wonderful Life* takes place over a twenty-five to thirty-year period, and the story occurs during various seasons, the layout must accommodate those changes as well, moving from season to season in a realistic manner. Scenes often change quickly within the film and Juniper recognizes the challenges that exist.

One specific challenge will be the creation of the trees that line the parkway along Genesee Street, as they are deciduous trees and will require the ability to grow and lose their leaves from scene to scene. Another issue is the snow that will cover the entire landscape during the winter scenes. It must appear in one scene almost instantaneously and in synchrony with the film, only to magically disappear in the next.

Juniper discovers a model maker in Fort Wayne, Indiana, who has successfully created model trees that contract their foliage into bladders beneath their trunks to simulate trees in winter. But when compressed, a leaf-like substance extrudes up through the trunk and out through the limbs until the tree appears lush with foliage. The leaves required by Juniper are monochromatic, so there is no need to change their color in autumn or spring. The main challenge will be the coordination involved in activating the transition among hundreds of deciduous trees so they can make the transition as a single unit.

The snow created for the scenes in *It's a Wonderful Life* was a technical marvel of its time and, based on the snow, the film received the Oscar for Best Special Effects at the 1947 Academy Awards celebration. Though much of the movie was modeled on snowy winters in the northeast, the movie was actually filmed on a backlot in southern California during the summer months in temperatures that on many days exceeded 90 degrees. Producing and removing snow for Juniper's model presented new challenges, since seasonal changes in the film were often conveying a lapse in time, with snow appearing rapidly over the winter landscape and then disappearing as the action moves to the spring or summer months.

In the early 2000s, a super-absorbant polymer was developed by the Japanese to keep babies' diapers dry, a side benefit of which was the creation of Insta-Snow, a white powder that, when mixed with water, grows many times its original size into a fluffy, white, snow-like substance. Juniper experimented with the polymer, shaking it through various meshes of fiberglass screening while misting it with water as it fell through. After several attempts, he found it possible to simulate an even and regulated snowfall that could cover trees, rooftops and all forms of solid terrain. Dry to the touch after setting, removal of the snow could be accomplished by sucking the powder into collection bags suspended from the ceiling using a cold ash vacuum system coupled with industrial mufflers to quiet the sucking noise and motor sounds of the system. Surprisingly, after several tries, no snow particles or residue remained. The only issue was that other small particles, such as ground cover and loose debris, could also be sucked into the equipment. Realizing this, Juniper specified aircraft adhesive to be used for the installation of all small parts and particles attached to structures, vehicles and people. The upside was that the remaining model received a good cleaning after cycling through the seasons.

From what Juniper finds online, no model maker has yet attempted the task he is taking on. As his project continues to grow in complexity, he is forced to embrace myriad new challenges. Each day he becomes newly aware of seemingly impossible tasks to be accomplished.

At night his anxiety worsens, as his head spins with ideas, making sleep difficult until he gains solace in a partial answer to a problem. That allows him to rest until morning, when he bounds up the steps two at a time to the second floor to work out an idea.

Leonder, though in daily contact with her husband, is happy she has not yet been asked to travel eastward. Living with Juniper is often like being in a beehive, making sleeping in the same bed sometimes impossible.

His mind never switches off, as even in sleep he tosses and turns, often speaking gibberish. She hopes that he will find peace with his project, but in her heart she knows that for every problem he solves, he will always find ten more to replace it.

Separate bedrooms might be the key when she moves east to Indiana. But for the moment, though missing him and his creative mind, she personally feels restored, and derives satisfaction from her own modest creations without enduring the frustrating challenges he faces and carries with him daily.

"I love him dearly," she thinks as she gets ready for bed. "I just don't know if I can continue to live with him."

Chapter Fifteen
The Documentary

Independent documentary film directors Elan Muzak and Kathleen Voight were invited guests of Pittsburgh Mayor Charles Nelson Taft for Juniper's presentation of his railroad concept to the city. Like many in the auditorium, they embraced Juniper's enthusiasm, if not his focus, as he spun the tale of creating an attraction for Pittsburgh that would rival those existing in major cities around the world. The directors were not surprised to learn a few days later that the project with the city had fallen through, but were even more surprised when Juniper surfaced again with a whole new idea for the lightly populated county of Indiana.

In their twenty-two years in the industry the team of Muzak & Voight have stumbled upon countless showboaters promoting grand plans they can't convert into workable projects. Usually they could see signs early on in a presentation or during the Q & A that the concept was ill-formed and hollow beneath a slick veneer. Juniper possessed some of the hallmarks of those entrepreneurial jesters. He was a hobbyist, not a professional, and from what they later discovered on the internet, besides his own personal model railroad, he had no credentials related to project planning or production in his resumé. He had no education or experience in production design, film production, script writing, cinematography, or editing. He had studied neither architecture nor city planning in college. He had never previously coordinated any project of note or worked with a team of collaborators except as a member of a group directed by others. He wasn't an entrepreneur, in that he has worked at Enstro Technologies as an AI fact checker for the past several years and never owned or managed a business.

Despite Juniper's obvious inexperience, there was something they saw in his plan that they liked. He was genuine, passionate and responded well to questions, so after being informed about a variation of his Pittsburgh proposal to the Indiana County Tourist Bureau, they finagled an invitation to the upcoming presentation to hear more about his proposal and to meet Juniper. As always, both Muzak and Voight had their enhanced cellular video cameras with them to record his speech.

As the team expected, the meeting goes well and they have time during this smaller venue to approach Juniper and explain to him that they are documentary film producers who have partnered on several projects over the years. Juniper is impressed by their credentials, and has even watched the documentary they produced for the Scientific American channel on tardigrades, the tiny, nearly indestructible animals that remain the only creatures from Earth to survive outer space.

When asked about his chances of getting a project for Indiana County commissioned, Juniper's answer is honest and to the point. "They need an attraction, and I have proposed a project that answers their needs. I have even provided possible sources of funding. It's now in their hands. Where it goes from here is up to them. I can't force my concept on them. I can only work with what they've got, and try my best to make it succeed."

"Have you, or have they, put together any focus groups, or surveyed the successes or failure rates of projects like yours in other cities? Do you have statistics to support your claims?"

"My profession is fact checking, and that's what I do to assure that AI has the best information available before it makes decisions. I have access to more data than most anyone in the country, if not the world, literally at my fingertips. What I don't know, I can usually find. So if you asked me about the top five attractions in the world, I would be able to provide financials, attendance records, and changes in demographics over any number of years, on most any themed event, movie, play, concert, or favorite food in less than a half hour. What I can't do is predict that which has never been done. I am not a charlatan or a mystic. I am a 34-year -old man who believes that he can create a single or multiple group of attractions that will accomplish a goal set by a group of people who could use my help. I can't guarantee that anything I do will be 100% successful. But from what I have researched, I know that I am not too far off the mark with my assumptions. I also know that Indiana County could spend all of its money on research without a tangible outcome. I'm willing to take a chance if they are, and my chance will cost them little and gain them a great deal of attention."

"If this concept is embraced by Indiana, would you consider allowing us to follow you on your journey?"

"In what way?"

"If the county and borough accept your proposal, would you mind if we took video of your progress during the process?" says Voight.

"I'd have to think about that. My processes are a little scattered at times."

"That's what we find fascinating about you, Juniper," says Muzak. "We have no idea what you're going to do. We don't know if you'll succeed or fail. We don't know whether the project will even be interesting to people. Even after hearing your plans, we know almost nothing about your project."

"We do need to admit to you that we captured footage of your presentation in Pittsburgh... and also tonight," says Voight. "Just in case something comes of the project."

"Would I get to view what you have so far and will be recording, as well as any drafts before you edit your film for public distribution?" asks Juniper.

"Of course," answers Voight. "If you aren't happy with the results, you'll have a right of refusal...but in the event that you do not succeed, and you allow us to produce it anyway, we'll guarantee that you'll get a percentage of any profits made from the film."

"You're telling me that you don't care if I succeed or not?"

"In a way it doesn't matter to us, but either way Indiana and The Jimmy Stewart Museum could succeed in getting their stories told, and if we make money, they'll make money, as will you," adds Muzak.

"That's the way it usually works when filming a documentary of this kind," he continues. "We have to first make a good story from the footage we capture, and the interviews we hold. We'll be filming both your struggles and successes, and we'll be rooting for you. But we only win if our film is captivating to watch, and if you, your topic and your story are interesting to an audience. And right now, we're interested in you."

"Will you interfere with my process as I work?"

"As little as possible," answers Voight. "The less we interfere the better."

"We will be interviewing other people to hear what they are thinking," adds Muzak.

"Will you tell me what they think?" asks Juniper.

"No. That would be interruptive to your process. We'll just be recording what happens, not affecting change," says Voight. "But we'll want to tag along to meetings, social functions, even some personal moments, and record you working through the process. We'll get approvals from anyone we use in the film, so that's not your worry."

"Do I need to talk to a lawyer, an agent, or someone else about my agreement with you?" asks Juniper.

Muzak smiles. "So far, you've been doing a pretty good job talking for yourself. We've been impressed with how you got this far with the little bit of credibility you have. We're rather amazed at your success."

"What if the project takes longer than I think it will to complete? What if after I am through, there's more that the town of Indiana wants to do to promote itself?" asks Juniper.

"We'll stay on the job as long as needed, or until the story is told to our liking. We may add an epilogue down the road to let people know what happens after our story ends, but otherwise, once we're done, we're done."

"Have you spoken to Faye or Nancy about this?"

"We've mentioned the idea," says Muzak.

"And...?" asks Juniper.

"Frankly, they're both intrigued by the idea. They see it as a 'win-win' for the county and the museum. In fact, it may have solidified support for your proposal."

"If I don't succeed, I could look like a fool," says Juniper.

"If you don't succeed, you'll look like a fool anyway. But if we succeed and you don't, you'll be a wealthier man than you would be if we don't succeed," responds Voight.

"If we all succeed, then it becomes a bigger payday for you, since your story will be promoted around the world, and every city planner in every country will come to you for a similar kind of project," adds Muzak.

"Let me see whether my project is approved," says Juniper. "Then let's see if we can work this out at the beginning without a contract."

"None?" asks Muzak.

"You want me to trust you," answers Juniper. "I think I trust you more without a contract than with one. If I get approval, and it looks like things are working okay, then we'll sit down and talk percentages."

"Okay! We'll do it your way. If we agree, will you let us begin filming?"

"A soon as I get approval. But you can also use any recordings you've filmed so far. A deal?"

"A deal!"

Chapter Sixteen
Just Wingin' It

As summer turns to fall, all that Juniper can focus on is how he is going to get enough done on this Bedford Falls model to have his prototype layout completed for the Christmas holiday in Indiana. The second floor of The Jimmy Stewart Museum has been closed off from visitors since May. Though stories continue to circulate about the progress of the model, the only people permitted entry are Juniper, the model makers, scenic designers, local volunteers, lighting specialists, the museum staff, the documentary film crew and the architects from the firm of Knowlton & Gidday.

The town of Bedford Falls has taken shape in that the majority of the buildings lining the parkway have been completed along with the Bedford Falls train station and a few of the homes and businesses of the characters featured in the film. The microbots have not yet arrived, nor has the guidance system that will synchronize their action with the film.

Miniature evergreen trees, and hedges of boxwood, leylandii, holly, and mountain laurel are crated each day and stored on the first floor of the museum, as well as several varieties of deciduous trees including maples, popular, black walnut and ash, plus the oaks that will line the parkway along Genesee Street. Much to Juniper's delight, the snow falling and removal system and the leaf growing and extraction processes are proving to work well, and the sections of layout devoted to the test scene scheduled for unveiling the weekend after Thanksgiving are beautifully crafted and keep expectations high for other structures yet to be built. The prototype thus far takes up approximately 2,500 square feet of space with room to grow as necessary. Monitors have been installed along all of the walls, and visitor pathways are being prepared for carpet, stainless steel rails and acrylic shielding.

Walls not used for backdrops of the Indiana borough and the countryside will display some of the concept drawings produced under Juniper's direction by the design team. A photographic story of the construction of other buildings displayed on the layout include the Bailey family home, the Bedford Falls station, and the downtown shops and businesses as viewed during the 10-minute segment developed and previewed over the holidays. Martini's Bar and the toll bridge located along Bridge Street will also be on view though not featured on the layout.

Other photos will include the interior of the miniature version of Gower's Drug Store and the office of Henry Potter, currently being made by model makers for display in shadow boxes that will line the walls as the construction continues over the next few years.

Juniper realizes that the second floor space will not accommodate too much expansion, so the model is created in sections that can be transported to a larger display venue in the future, to eventually be part of an expanded version of the layout. Though he has already conceived of what that enlargement might include, he is reluctant to divulge expansion plans prior to the launch of the *It's a Wonderful Life* segment already in progress.

Although Juniper has moved into the temporary first floor quarters established for him by the museum, he has not had time to search for a more permanent residence, and Leonder has only visited her husband once since he left Erran Heights. Balancing the project with his job has proven difficult, but balancing it with his marriage may be impossible. It is only through the kindness of his boss at Enstro that he can support himself and his wife while devoting the hours necessary to manage all of the details surrounding the model's development.

Fortunately, Faye and Nancy have proven to be staunch allies, and together have raised more than $1.5 million from grants and private donors to keep construction moving at an accelerated pace. Details of the project have been leaked to the press, but the overall concept has been glossed over since no one, including Juniper, knows exactly what the final outcome will be.

Falon, who has already taken a shuttle to the Jimmy Stewart Airport several times, arrives on a golden September day to view the progress status and to provide Juniper with needed input. After seeing the status of the layout, he asks Juniper exactly what he's planned for those segments of the layout not central to the action, the script or the story.

"Looks like there will be a lot of empty space," observes Falon.

Since Juniper has focused primarily on the 10-minute segment comprising the test scene, he has not bothered much with the day-to-day activities of the community, such as the nightly crowd at Martini's Bar, Mary's job searches or pastimes, the mergers and financial dealings of Henry Potter, or the negotiations between customers and management at the Bailey Building and Loan, when they are not of primary interest in the film.

"Unfortunately, your model consists of the entire community, and the action can't just stop and be cut as it does in the movie. People must live their lives, go shopping, attend meetings and meet up for lunch or a matinee at the Bijou.

"I love where you've taken the project thus far," admits Falon. "But there are some questions that have to be dealt with such as Genesee Street, which turns into a "den of iniquity" during the fantasy segment depicting Bedford Falls *if* George Bailey had never existed."

"I have addressed the transformation of Genesee Street. That's been the most fun of all. It involves turning a barber shop into a pool hall and fight arena, one of the cafés into the Blue Moon Bar, with the Bijou Theatre transforming into a strip club, an antique shop becoming the Bamboo Room, and a floral shop becoming a pawnbroker. Most notable is the change of the Bailey Building and Loan to the Midnight Club, a dime-a-dance parlor, if George had never been born to fight for its preservation."

Juniper explains that during the fantasy sequence new facades and signage will pop up from the sidewalk, accompanied by a wild jazz score meant to emphasize the degradation of the community from one of family values to that of a honky-tonk town as George confronts his alternative past as presented by Clarence, the angel.

"What happens elsewhere during that scene?" asks Falon.

"I'm not sure yet," admits Juniper. "But we know that if George Bailey never existed, Mary becomes a spinster working at the Pottersville Public Library, George's mother turns her home into a boarding house, and Bailey Park becomes the cemetery where Harry Bailey's body is buried because George wasn't born to save his brother from drowning."

"And how are you going to make sense of all these changes, Juniper? How will anyone maintain a focus on the story with all that you envision happening during Clarence's alternative story?"

"I don't know, Falon.

"I won't be sure how any of it will fit together until I'm ready to address the issues one at a time."

"You do have a plan, right?"

"Sort of!" admits Juniper.

"It's the way I work best, Falon. If I tried to address everything ahead of time, I'd never get the project completed."

Standing in the middle of the second floor of The Jimmy Stewart Museum, Juniper extends his lower arms bent at the elbows with his palms pointed towards the ceiling and makes a stationary spin that encompasses the room. "Here's my plan today... all of it. Tomorrow it may be something else. Yesterday it was something... other. Each day is like that for me. I lose my wallet, mislay my keys, and make new plans based on what just happened. The microbots aren't ready, but they must be soon. If not, I will have a different plan."

"You know that you sound insane, Juniper. Do Faye and Nancy know that you're winging it?"

"I don't think they care. But my answer to you is this: What does it matter how I get the job done, as long as I get the job done? I work around obstacles, and am not impeded by them. They are part of my process."

"What if everyone worked that way?" asks Falon.

"Everyone can't work that way," answers Juniper. "And I can't work any other way. Look around you. Am I making progress?"

"Yes, it's quite impressive, especially since you have no idea what you're doing."

"It's not that bad. I have a general idea. Tomorrow we will turn autumn to winter and then to spring at the touch of a button, and snow will fall on Bedford Falls, coating the streets, homes and terrain. What's not possible one day becomes reality the next. That's what people like about the story of *It's a Wonderful Life.* Anything is possible, and sorrow can be replaced by happiness at the ringing of a bell, or a change of heart. Why should I restrict what I do because of factors over which I have no control?"

"Okay, Juniper. I don't understand or agree, but I see your point. What's next?"

"If all goes well, we'll have the first microbots by the beginning of next week. Until then, we'll work out details such as the electromagnetic track embedded in the streets, and the programming of the cars and other vehicles. Once the first section is completed, the others will follow along as simply variations of the one created before it."

"And you'll make the November 26th deadline for the prototype debut?" asks Falon.

"As long as the microbots are delivered by next week, we're good!"

A cinematographer and videographer have digitally captured the exchange between Juniper and Falon from different angles, along with clips of the model layout and Juniper spinning around with his arms extended like Christ at the Sea of Galilee. After the exchange, they collect some final shots for their "B" roll of the photographs and graphics on the wall, and the spaces where buildings are yet to be placed.

When the shoot is completed, the cinematographer contacts Kathleen Voight, and summarizes the exchange between Juniper and Falon.

"He actually admitted that he has no plan?" Kathleen questions.

"Yep. No coherent plan. He seems to believe that his plan will develop on its own."

"How does it look, so far?"

"He's making progress. People are working, walls are going up, and the layout is expanding. The way that I see it, he does have a plan, but it's flexible and he doesn't want it to get in the way of his forward momentum," says the videographer. "Juniper's like an orchestra leader without a score in front of him, and the musicians are seeing and hearing only their parts of the music for the first time. The music that comes out is structured, but also organic in that none of the musicians know exactly what the composition is supposed to sound like. The orchestra leader is confident as he directs the strings, horns, flutes and drums, and loves the music he hears, but also knows that it may not be as intended by the composer."

"That's the way Juniper works," states Kathleen, matter-of-factly.

"Yep."

"What a ride this will be!" concludes Kathleen.

Chapter Seventeen
The Stars of the Show

The microbots don't arrive the following week... or the week after. Sayre isn't responding to calls or messages and Juniper can't move much further on the prototypical scene without the figurines. But the following Tuesday several packages arrive at the museum from M-Bots along with a note from Sayre:

"Hope this is worth all of the angst. Not sure how we can get paid for all that's been done, but nothing ventured...well, you know the rest."

The crates that arrive are numbered, as are the boxes inside each crate, which are made of heavy gray card stock with a peach-colored foam insert that encases each figure. A hard copy of the manual is enclosed in a separate box on the top layer of crate number one. It is accompanied by a complete list of the figurines within each crate, keyed by box number, with a brief description of each character's role in the film.

George Bailey is listed as item number one, but instead of finding one George Bailey, Juniper finds several versions, each labeled with the scene or scenes in which the character appears, and dressed to correspond with the outfit worn in the film. A small envelope is taped to the box and labeled *To Juniper,* and inside is a hand-printed note from Sayre:

You may not need all of the George Baileys at this time, but once we made one... we made them all.

No other characters arrive with multiples outfits, but all of the characters for the test scene are represented, including Ruth, Vi, Ma Bailey, Harry Bailey, Mary, three porters, the crowd on Genesee Street and several others Juniper couldn't figure out, but which have descriptions and are dressed and made up to match the fashion of the on-screen actors.

Each character weighs about 6 ounces, with most of the mass relegated to the legs and mid-section for stability, and each is accompanied by instructions for layout placement, body movements possible, and easy-to-follow descriptions for modifications of preprogrammed functions.

After all of the boxes are removed from the crates, a final note lays at the bottom in a large white envelope:

Much of what we have built into the figures was never asked for, but is necessary. You'll realize the enormity of the task when you start populating your model and assembling the scene. More characters will be on their way shortly.

You never could have put together the vast model you proposed to Pittsburgh, even with my help. We both know that. The manual should be complete, and the functionality of the figurines robust and magical enough to turn heads, blow minds, and inspire new ideas. Best of luck with your prototype. I look forward to viewing it at the museum at the opening this holiday season.

John

Within two weeks, Juniper's team incorporated all of the figurines into the test segment, as well as the additional figures provided, but not requested. Using the manual and noted instructions from Sayre, the team, composed mostly of volunteers, is able to coordinate the movements of the figures with the actions of the characters presented in the original film, as well as provide non-interruptive movement and actions to other parts of the layout. The documentary film crew records each segment on the model from multiple angles, including aerial views, and Juniper, with the permission of Muzak and Voight, integrates a portion of the footage into Capra's film, extending and modifying scenes to correspond with the activity on the model.

On his first viewing of the completed scene, Juniper becomes aware of his dependence on Sayre and Sayre's company, and the extraordinary achievement accomplished, because the characters move with an ease and fluidity he never imagined. Without his friend's effort, and his willingness to put conflicts aside, Juniper would surely have failed. Though Sayre had been impudent in stealing away the Pittsburgh project, Juniper was also blinded by his own delusions, which surpassed his ability to produce what he had promised.

In an attempt to make amends, he drafts a note to Sayre and sends it shortly after viewing the preliminary cut.

Dear John,

It seems that there are times in our lives when some of us think ourselves the master of the universe, and that all that we imagine can be achieved by our own doing. As my crew and I have worked with your microbots, and I have witnessed the level of achievement capable by you and your engineers, I have realized just how limited I have been in my thinking, and just how lucky I am to have your support on this project.

Despite what you write about making a profit, there is no doubt in my mind that you will gain greatly from the technology you've created, and are already looking ahead to applications derived from your achievement for industry, medicine and space exploration. If you had been a different kind of person, you might have continued to battle me and have succeeded. But, by being smarter than I am, you used your advantage positively, not to defeat me, but to make my concept a reality.

For that I thank you.

Humbly yours,
Juniper

Within an hour of sending the message to Sayre, Juniper receives a response.

Dear Juniper,

Your talents are different than mine. You have the ability to conceive from thin air while I depend on the realities of our time to build anything. I was wrong to have challenged your authority on the Pittsburgh project. The vision was grand and beautiful, but at the time I couldn't imagine how you could possibly pull it together on your own, and used the advantage to make my own a dream we shared, but one that depended on brick and mortar, and not on lofty thoughts as you proposed.

In many ways, the Indiana project you've taken on is far more difficult than an historic recreation, yet your mind soars past obstacles like a stealth aircraft avoids detection. You can change any idea on a dime, and leave us, who rely on technology and reality, in the dust.

I do believe you would find it difficult to do this project without me, but there are other engineers and technology companies you would have found. Though borderline insane, you are also unique, and I am happy that I can be a part of your journey.

> *Fondly,*
> *John*

Chapter Eighteen
The Big Reveal

Friday, November 26 is the date set for the first public viewing of the ten minute segment of *It's a Wonderful Life in Miniature*. A "By Invitation Only" preview event is scheduled for the Saturday before the Thanksgiving holiday. Announcements were released to the press the last week in October.

Though not scheduled for completion until the second week in November, the prototype merging of the movie and the model has exceeded Juniper's expectations. Faye, Nancy, and the head of the Board of Directors of The Jimmy Stewart Museum have already viewed the program and can barely keep silent about the multiple amazing features of the project.

In addition to the O-gauge layout, which occupies 4,200 square feet of floor space, dimensional display boxes lining one wall reveal the interiors of Gower's Drug Store, the Bailey living room decorated for the holidays, Henry Potter's office, the high school gym and swimming pool, and the toll bridge booth. All were constructed and decorated by model makers from Indiana County and installed in the museum during the first week in November.

The segment captured from Capra's original movie has been altered by RealView Video and preserves the original aspect ratio of 1.37:1, but displays the film in ultra-high definition 8K format. Each frame in the segment was enlarged using AI editing capabilities, which adds details lost in the original film. Custom-built 48-inch monitors provided by Sony retain the integrity of the black and white film while increasing the overall quality of the production. The revised score has been recorded by the Pittsburgh Symphony Orchestra to include new orchestrations based on Dimitri Tiomkin's themes. One notable inclusion is an accordion, Jimmy Stewart's childhood instrument, to provide the backdrop for George Bailey's walk to Genesee Street from his mother's house following Harry's Welcome Home party. Though only a small segment of the film will be shown at this time, the complete score, as performed by the Pittsburgh Symphony Orchestra, will be released by Sony and will be available exclusively from the museum prior to the completion of the project, now scheduled for the following November.

News of the animated figures has not been released since the tourism bureau and museum board hope to keep the use of microbots from going public prior to the Press Preview. *60 Minutes* correspondent Poppy Hager has already approached the museum about doing a feature, and has requested an invitation for herself and her film crew for a private preview. Once video of the test segment is released to the press and uploaded to YouTube, the board of the Stewart Museum expects the exhibit to be the premier attraction throughout the 2060 holiday season.

The construction period was shortened due to the dedication of the model makers, as well as M-Bots, Knowlton & Gidday, the Indiana Chamber of Commerce and the board of directors of both the tourism bureau and The Jimmy Stewart Museum. Most of the buildings and locations presented in the film were completed prior to October, including the toll bridge and canal where George Bailey and Clarence first meet, the school gym, and the drafty old Granville Mansion that George and Mary occupy after they are married.

At the southern end of the model, past a wooded area and a few residential streets, stands a reproduction of the Dutch Colonial home on Vinegar Hill owned by Stewart's parents, where the actor grew up from the age of five. The house looks out over the Indiana borough as it has for nearly 150 years, and is located just a few blocks north of Philadelphia Street. A diorama of that main thoroughfare includes the rear of the Stewart Museum and provides context for the location of Bedford Falls, just a whistle stop away from the Indiana borough. Though the proximity of Bedford Falls to Indiana is a fabrication contrived by Juniper, it is no greater stretch of the imagination than the assumption that Jimmy Stewart was Capra's inspiration for the character of George Bailey when he began creating the film that was based on Philip Van Doren Stern's original story, *The Greatest Gift.* Indiana, like Seneca Falls, New York, another town claiming ownership of Bedford Falls, was a composite of small-town America in the first half of the 20th century, and was promoted as a place of opportunity where a boy like Jimmy, the son of a hardworking store owner, could then be educated at Princeton University and go on to become a war hero and a celebrity recognized the world over.

THE PREVIEW

The monitors surrounding the second floor gallery of the museum remain dark, as the ceiling fills with planets and constellations. Two stars in the center flicker as they speak back and forth to each other discussing George Bailey's future.

The morning sun becomes visible on the eastern wall of the gallery. The pitch of a whistle rises as a 2-4-4-2 engine chugs along the rails and rounds the bend to the Bedford Falls station. Figures of George Bailey and

Uncle Billy on the model are revealed by a spotlight above them; they are not yet visible on the monitors still glowing with the constellations. George, the taller and thinner figure, is recognizably a miniature version of Jimmy Stewart. He is reviewing brochures, while an older man next to him in a white suit is listening to the young man's ramblings and responding. The two are surrounded by people scurrying to and from the station. Porters are busying themselves in preparation for toting bags and crates to cars and wagons. Other characters are seen chatting amiably while waiting for the train to arrive.

The engine's whistle blasts a final time as the train arrives. Then Harry emerges from a passenger car, fresh from college, and the scene from the original film is picked up on the monitor. Harry introduces Ruth, his new wife, to his brother while friends and family gather around him bestowing greetings. He explains to George his plan to *not* come home permanently and take over the building and loan, but to move on to Buffalo to work as an analyst in his father-in-law's glass factory.

Ruth and George talk and then day darkens to night on both the model and the screen, and a spotlight captures the Welcome Home party at Ma Bailey's house. George speaks to his mother about his dreams and about Mary, a childhood friend who's returned home from school, and then he strolls downtown to Genesee Street, where he sweet-talks the town flirt, Vi, without success, and then heads off in the opposite direction towards Mary's house.

Some of the action on the model remains invisible to the audience because it takes place indoors, but the monitors surrounding the layout show the characters' shadows cast on the walls and window shades of the interiors. Juniper has tested each scene multiple times with the lighting and technical crews to achieve the optimal blending of scenes that when finalized will be uploaded to digital drives on the computer for replay. Reactions from test audiences further refine the staging, as movements of individuals and groups are viewed from multiple angles and vantage points within the gallery. It had never been Juniper's intention to provide only one viewing perspective; he wants secondary points of interest enabling visitors to return time and time again without becoming tired of the presentation.

Over the course of the few months that Juniper's worked with the micro-bots, he's become more aware of their capabilities as well as the challenges, limitations and the possibilities for developing parallel plot lines for most every scene.

Sayre at one point sends Juniper a microbot dog and tells him to use it however he believes it best fits within the model. Juniper replies that he also needs a postman, so Sayre has an outfit stitched and sent out overnight. The next day, Juniper has the tiny postman delivering the mail to Ma Bailey's neighbor. He is then chased by the dog to Vi's house, and she lets him in. Juniper adds the postman episode to the opening scene at the station wondering if and when someone will notice the implied sexual liason. Nobody notices it, so he adds a few more parallel episodes prior to completion.

With the preview approaching, Juniper has little time to find a temporary residence for himself and Leonder in the Indiana borough. Leonder refuses to visit again until he finds living quarters better than the first floor office of the museum. Then the Tourist Bureau comes through with the offer of a corporate-owned suite reserved for visiting dignitaries in a building near the tracks on Philadelphia Street. It has a full kitchen, a whirlpool tub in the bath and a large living room. They offer it to the couple for a three-week stay beginning the week before Thanksgiving and ending three days after the public viewing.

Leonder agrees to take a shuttle to Indiana and attend the functions surrounding the unveiling, even though she's found it much more comfortable and calm at their home in Crestoria without Juniper around.

She arrives two days prior to the event, and reads, shops and takes long naps while Juniper finalizes tests on the model. Juniper is well aware that his obsession with the project has damaged his relationship with his wife, but he also recognizes that doors that will open for him if this project is successful. He has already spoken to Sayre about possible partnership ventures together. Leonder doesn't care to listen to Juniper's dreams. For her, she sees only nightmares of futile activities in which she will play no part and in which she will receive little notice or be of any significance. After her arrival in Indiana, she remains polite and smiles at everyone she meets, but she neither grasps Juniper's motivation, nor truly wants any involvement. She had thought that the ground floor train layout in their pod in Crestoria would satisfy Jupitor's need for a personal world, and that movie night with friends would fulfill his desire to live in the past, but these activities appeared only to elevate his anxiety and his need for goals that seem unattainable.

The model has not only taken over the couple's lives but is threatening Juniper's job. His boss has spoken to Leonder with concerns about her husband's performance of late. She worries that he'll lose his income. Her pottery is for the most part a hobby, so the couple's existence is dominated by pastimes rather than work. She has no way of communicating her fears to her husband as he is living in his private dream world... one she fears he may never give up.

Juniper plans an evening out. The Pittsburgh Symphony Orchestra is performing a holiday program at Indiana University and he has tickets. It will be preceded by dinner at Boxer's, the nicest restaurant in the borough. He tells her to dress up for the evening, and arrives at their suite early with a bouquet of red roses in a vase and ready for display. He has also brought along a bottle of champagne and a selection of fancy hors d'oeuvres.

She smiles when he hands her the gifts, and he gets down on one knee, puts his hands together and tells her how much she means to him. He makes no excuses, but apologizes sincerely for...*everything!*

He knows what he's doing to us, she thinks. Then says, "Why....?"

He interrupts with, "If this project comes to nothing, I won't look for others. I will content myself with the life I have and dedicate myself to being a good husband, friend and worker. If something does come out of all of this, I won't let it rule me, and I will consult with you about how we can best share our life together."

Nice words, she thinks, knowing he will never change. So as to not ruin the evening, she holds her tongue rather than scream, and they head out for their date night with no resolution to their issues. Despite his promises, Juniper remains distracted. The model is his mistress, and Leonder is relegated to the role of the devoted wife. I have options, she thinks, as they finish dessert and head off to the concert. I have options.

Chapter Nineteen
The Reaction

On Saturday evening the board members of The Jimmy Stewart Museum, the Indiana Chamber of Commerce and the Indiana Tourist Board, reporters from local and national news networks, and special invited guests meet in the third floor galleries of the museum at a reception for the debut of a short segment of *It's a Wonderful Life in Miniature*. After all guests are checked in and have a chance to chat, and grab a glass of wine and an appetizer, Stewart Museum Executive Director Faye Gunther herds the crowd into the main gallery and introduces Nancy Boyle and Juniper Blakely to the audience.

Faye speaks of Nancy and her meeting with Juniper in Pittsburgh, during which Nancy urged him to develop a tourist attraction for Indiana to rival those of large cities. The town needed something that would reinvigorate enthusiasm for Jimmy Stewart and introduce a new dimension of entertainment to the world. She is clear in her message as she tells the audience that what they are about to see is just a short segment of a much longer presentation planned for the following Christmas season. She concludes by saying that they are fortunate to have Juniper onboard and working with a talented team of local model makers, artists and technology experts to assemble the prototype to be previewed on the floor below.

There is a smattering of applause after which Juniper is asked to say a few words.

"I believe that most of you are familiar with *It's a Wonderful Life*, starring Indiana's hometown hero, Jimmy Stewart. The movie was released at Christmas 114 years ago and has been a favorite ever since. Faye and Nancy invited me to re-envision it from a unique perspective for a new audience in a new way. The exhibit you will see is a work in progress and is based on a railroad spur line that actually ran through Indiana for more than 150 years. The model layout you will see portrays the Borough of Indiana as it looked from the 1920s to the 1950s, only a whistle stop away from the fictional town of Bedford Falls.

"As Faye stated in her introduction, this evening's segment uses new technology, but also the talents of hundreds of artisans, film editors and technologists from the area to reimagine the story in a physical form. But then the monitors will also show existing footage from the film merged with new footage from the model.

"Though you will be introduced to the production, I repeat what Faye has said, that it is only a small segment of the show planned for next season. We hope what you see tonight will inspire you to return with family and friends next November!

"There are two ways to descend to the second floor, the first by the small elevator, and the other using the stairs. If you can negotiate the stairs, please do. I sincerely hope you have a wonderful experience!"

After a few moments, volunteers direct the guests to the stairs and elevator which, because of its small size, can only handle ten people at a time. Several people who are waiting decide to take the stairs instead, and encounter gridlock at the entrance to the second floor display gallery.

Lights are dim, and there is some confusion as to where to stand. A few people prefer to sit, which makes it more difficult for them to see the model, and each takes up the space of two or three people standing.

Despite the absence of light, those people following the path through the exhibit are able to note the complexity of the layout and begin pointing out buildings and areas they recognize in both Indiana and the fictional town of Bedford Falls. Juniper notes how tight the space is for the visitors and wonders whether, despite all of his planning, there is enough room for everyone to follow the action.

When all are settled, the exhibition opens to the night sky, two blinking and talking stars, and a planetarium-like view of the cosmos. Ten minutes later the program concludes, after which Faye explains the museum's plans for the project's completion. At that point she asks for questions.

Several hands raise, and the first is from an older man picked by Faye. "Where's the snow? Where was Clarence? What scene were we watching and why does it look like summer?"

Faye starts to explain again that this is only a short segment of the full exhibition and features a scene that appears earlier in the film, when a young woman raises her hand. Juniper calls on her. "I like the town, and I love the miniature people. They're so much fun to watch, but, yes, where is the snow? Wasn't *It's a Wonderful Life* a Christmas film? And there aren't any children in the scene."

An African-American reporter from the *Baltimore Sun* calls out, "I counted only four black people in the layout. Didn't any more black people live in Indiana or Bedford Falls back in the day? How do I get to Bedford Falls from here? It looks like a nice town to visit."

A middle-aged woman on the tourism board raises her hand and states, "I watch the film every year, but I don't remember that scene at all. Why isn't it Christmassy? Why is it all in black and white?"

A member of the chamber of commerce jumps into the conversation, "I see you have the bridge over here," he says pointing to it. "Can we see Clarence, or isn't he ready yet?"

The documentary film crew is trying to hold its laughter in while it records the chaos of the questioning as the Q&A segment unravels before them. There are no answers that will please those asking the questions, and the questions keep coming. Juniper tries to explain the absence of snow, but nobody seems to understand that it doesn't snow in late summer in the northeast. The crowd seems more like a mob than invited guests as they continue their attack. Leonder, who's found a place in a corner, understands their confusion, but feels sympathy for her husband, who tries in vain to defend the segment and its significance within the film.

"The robots are amazing, and your transitions are extraordinary," calls out a young man about 20 years of age. "I love the fact that you brought Bedford Falls back to Indiana, and that I now know what the town looks like. It would be great if you could physically build the town here in Indiana County. I love it all. I can't wait to see the full show when it's completed."

With that reaction, the crowd simmers down, but many feel a bit claustrophobic and wish to exit, which is difficult because the entrance and exits are blocked by chairs. Faye and Nancy speak with many privately as they leave. Few talk with Juniper, but when they do, they seem like advocates. One reporter takes him aside and says, "This is an extraordinary achievement, young man. It could use a bigger venue, and has some rough spots, but overall, I think you are a visionary. Congratulations!"

Six of the reporters stick around for a second showing, selecting positions near the layout where they can get the optimal view. The six watch the action carefully, and several notice a few of the peripheral plot lines they missed during the first showing.

"Bravo!" says one at the end of the segment.

"Well done," says another.

The six show their approval with a burst of applause.

"Where do we go from here?" Faye asks Juniper.

Nancy jumps in with, "I'm not sure. I think we'll have to wait for the reviews."

"I think we already have witnessed our review," says Juniper, who looks past Nancy to see Leonder leaning against a wall, her face expressionless. She sees him and smiles wanly as she walks over to him.

"Not what I hoped for," says Juniper.

"What did you expect?" she asks.

"I wanted them to see what I've been seeing."

"So now you're prepared for the worst?"

Faye and Nancy walk over to the couple and Faye blurts out, "If only we had snow!"

Nancy adds, "People don't seem to remember much about the plot from year to year or decade to decade."

"They remember the bridge scene and Clarence," says Faye.

"People told me that they remember Martini's Bar, and the phone kiss between Mary and George, but neither of these scenes are in your segment," says Nancy to Juniper.

"What do we do? The public opening is a week away," Faye points out.

"I'll fix it!" says Juniper emphatically as he looks towards his wife, who knows all too well what that means.

"We'll have snow and the bridge scene by next Friday, but we have to limit each showing to 25 people."

Leonder has walked back to her corner. It's the week before Thanksgiving and the couple was planning to spend the holiday at home with friends, believing that Juniper would be done with the model layout for the time being.

"Can you do that?" asks Faye hopefully.

"I must, and I will," says Juniper as he walks over to Leonder and tries to comfort her.

"I know what you have to do," says Leonder. "There is no turning back. I don't like it, but I understand."

"But I promised you," Juniper reminds her.

"I can't change you, Juniper. There are parts of you I love dearly, and I admire you. What I prefer is irrelevant at this point, but I'll not be staying here this week. I'll be leaving tomorrow."

"Can we sort this out later?" asked Juniper.

"We can discuss things, if that's what you mean, but I'm not sure what purpose talk will serve for any of our issues."

"I need you, Leonder!"

"You need your dreams more than you need me," she says. "I can't hold that against you, but I also need things, and that may be hard for you to understand. Let's not talk about it now. You have work to get done. I'll see you at the suite."

Leonder goes to the third floor coat room via the elevator, and Juniper remains where he is and turns to view his creation. He knows what he needs to do, and there is little time to waste.

He puts in a call to John Sayre.

"How'd it go out there in Pennsylvania?" asks his friend.

"I need the toll taker... and Clarence as soon as possible. What can you do for me?"

"I already have them for you."

"You have what, John?"

"Clarence and the toll taker are done, completed and programmed."

"How did you know I needed them?" says Juniper.

"I didn't, but we had a few slow days, and I wanted to personally get a vision of Clarence. I also have Mary, if you need her, but not the Bailey children."

"How about the man whose tree George hits?"

"He's a generic character. We'll make his costume."

"Thanks, John!"

"So, Juniper. Do I seem a bit of an angel?"

"You're no Clarence, John, and you know it."

"No, but you definitely are a George Bailey," laughs Sayre.

Chapter Twenty
Juniper's Dilemma

Though his wife's departure hurts him to his core, Juniper knows what he must do to fix the preview's problems. The comments of the audience should have been predictable. Other than Faye's brief introduction and his remarks prior to the showing, the guests had little background upon which to base their opinions. To justify the train pulling into the Bedford Falls station, there was little or no context the visitors could possibly have had about the motivations of George and his brother, nor were they provided any references to the scene prior to the preview. He knows from his profession that people neither listen carefully, nor interpret quickly, so each person who voiced his or her opinion was reacting in a personal way. He should have anticipated that.

Though shocked by the response, Faye and Nancy may have always wondered about the absence of snow in the test segment, as well as Juniper's omission of the scenes most memorable in the minds of people who love the movie. To most who watch the film year after year, it's the emotion that gets to them, not the action and certainly not George's dreams of success. Capra had it right, and Juniper got it wrong in the first draft. But he can fix it.

The greater problem Juniper faces is the fission in his relationship with Leonder, and the promise he has already broken, one made just a few days after he had begged her forgiveness. He can't pretend it doesn't exist. Her points are valid, and here he is going full steam ahead, ignoring the Thanksgiving holiday, and proving that he is more concerned with his own ego and self-righteous responsibility than he is in his wife's happiness.

After being driven with his wife to the airport for her trip home aboard the shuttle, Juniper is immediately transported back to the museum to work on the winter snowfall and the bridge scene from the movie. There is no logical segue from one to the other, but that doesn't seem to matter to the public at this point. Before starting his work, he calls in several staff members and tells them the issues that need to be addressed, and that the robots of Clarence and a few other characters will be arriving with other packages on the afternoon drone delivery. He then receives a call from Faye.

Have you seen the reviews, Juniper? People have been emailing me since early morning. The New York Times, the Indiana Gazette, the Philadelphia Inquirer *and* the Washington Post *all praised your achievement. Even* the Baltimore Sun *endorsed it, although mentioning the scarcity of black characters, and how a few more added might benefit the project.*

"I don't understand, it seemed like they hated it," answers a bewildered Juniper.

"They just didn't understand it. We also had far too many people crowded in at one time. We may need a bigger place to display it in the future. A few papers weren't as gracious and spoke of the gallery as being cramped and uncomfortable, and the staging as "difficult to comprehend," but the major news sources seemed to love it, and also noted that what a visitor is seeing is just a small portion of the whole exhibition and *not* the entire performance."

"I've called Sayre and he's overnighting the Clarence figure to me," responds Juniper. "We will end with a snowfall and the bridge scene expected by yesterday's audience."

"But we thought you were going home for the holiday."

"I can't leave the program where it is," responds Juniper. "Especially now that I know that most people only value the experience if they get to see Bedford Falls in the snow, and George leaping into the canal. We may have to provide shorter segments over time, and save the full production for only special occasions in the future."

"So, you'll be staying in Indiana over the weekend?"

"I don't seem to have a choice. It's my responsibility to see the project through. I have some members of the team that live nearby and who can help me fix the problems, but I'll also need to be here to supervise them as well as prepare for the Friday showing."

"You're welcome to come to my house for dinner on Thursday. My children will be fascinated by your love of toy trains, and my husband is a classic movie buff, so you'll be the perfect guest. I'm also going to have my mother and sister over. Mom's a bit ditzy, somewhat like the people in the audience the other night who didn't get what you had done. She gets lost easily when it comes to technology, but she does love the film *It's a Wonderful Life.*"

"Thank you," says Juniper. "I'll most likely take you up on that offer. I feel awful about failing to be home with my wife. I've stayed away far too long."

Two of the local scenic designers arrive, and Juniper excuses himself from Faye and goes to the entrance to meet them. He explains his concerns and how he hopes to resolve them. They will need to complete the installation of the leaf retraction/extraction system for the layout, test it, and make sure that the snow vacuuming system works as efficiently as it did when it was first installed two months ago above mesh mounted to the ceiling. The second issue will be the canal water that flows under the toll bridge. Currently the water consists of epoxy resin and is not a liquid. Although the canal is deep enough to accommodate water or glycerin, no systems have been created as of yet to move the water or allow for the depth of Clarence's plunge, George's dive, or the manner in which the character rescues and swims Clarence to the shore. In the film, the water is churning quite rapidly, at a much greater rate than is probably possible in a canal, but that roiling of water is what is needed for the model. The depth drops significantly as it runs downstream. The challenge is to create a dense enough liquid to simulate the water at O-scale and make it flow downhill through the model to a pump that will bring the liquid back to the canal's origin. This is not a problem according to the scenic designers, but it is of concern to Juniper.

He knows that he alone has the ability to configure George's dive into the water, his grab for Clarence, and their swim to the shore line. Both characters will be wet, and both characters will need to be able to realistically climb up the side of the canal to the tollmaster's station. Juniper checks to make sure he has the correct George Bailey figure and that the figure is impervious to moisture and built for diving as well as swimming.

Juniper now opens the box inscribed *George Bailey on the Bridge*. Inside, he finds a heavier figure, dressed in the clothes George wore to Martini's Bar in the movie. On removing the character from its foam packaging, Juniper finds a note:

Hello, Juniper. I have no idea when you will get to the enclosed George figure who must save the life of Clarence, but you will need to have this information before activating it. This George Bailey is coated with a clear, flexible silicone, but its clothes aren't. The character can get wet and still function, and the figure is programmed to dive into the water only after the Clarence character jumps. When in the water, the Bailey figure will attach itself to the Clarence figure and swim with it to the shoreline. Once at the water's edge, the figures will separate, and will require onsite programming to climb to the bridge. You must leave time for this to happen, and also provide target points for both of them to sit within the tollmaster's booth. I have no idea of the distances on your layout at this point, or the speed at which the two characters can ascend. You may choose to fade to black, as they did in the film, which will disguise any awkward movements the characters may exhibit when climbing.

Please contact me when you need Clarence, or I will send him along after the holiday.

All my best,

John

Once again, Juniper is amazed at Sayre's anticipatory thinking, and wonders why John seems to have changed so much and been kinder following his attempted theft of Juniper's project in Pittsburgh. Since that time, Sayre has certainly come through for him over and over again in ways Juniper finds quite remarkable.

Next on Juniper's list is the music that follows the action of the tollmaster as he sweeps a light across the water from his place on the bridge. Since most of the scene will be visible on the monitors, and it ends shortly after Clarence is saved by George, there doesn't seem much music to be altered in the score, so Juniper needn't bother with that.

Juniper takes the stairs to Faye's fourth-floor office and provides an update. She gets up from her desk to greet him, conscious of the mission Juniper's on, as well as familiar with the conflicts he's facing with his wife, due in part to his responsibilities to the museum.

Juniper has little time for chit-chat and starts right in. "Here's what's going to happen this coming Friday, Faye. First, we must limit each viewing to a maximum of 25 people. At this point the entire program will last no longer than 13 minutes, efficiently allowing four groups an hour through the first evening's performance. That's a total of 100 people per hour. If the

It's a Wonderful Life – 2060

evening's events last 3 hours, that's 300 people. More might want to come, but you will need to provide alternative day or night hours for the viewings, and use the third floor gallery for the sale of T-shirts, posters, mugs and whatever else, as well as taking orders for the orchestration of the revised score, and the documentary still being developed."

"You think *too* many people will arrive?" asks Faye.

"I'm positive of it, but we can't miss this chance. If you are open eight hours on Saturday and eight hours on Sunday, over the three days you will accommodate 2,000 people."

As Faye and Juniper speak, the documentary film crew is recording their conversation while trying to keep pace with Juniper's team as they make changes to the layout. The filmmakers are on 24-hour duty, record during lunch and dinner breaks, and follow Juniper back to his suite each evening. Juniper has even allowed them access to his end of phone calls with Leonder as he tries to salvage their relationship.

After being up most of the previous night, at 10:00 AM on Thanksgiving Day, Juniper returns to his suite and watches the parade on the monitor in his room, and then tries several times to call Leonder... with no response. He heads off to Faye's house at 3:00 PM and meets her family. While waiting for dinner, Juniper plays with the kids and shows them a video of his train layout at home. Faye's mother is a bit disoriented, but funny, and her sister is lovely and kind to him. He wishes that Leonder would have joined him, but understands that he owns his problems, and can't expect forgiveness or grace from his wife at this juncture.

The Indiana holiday celebration will be held the following evening, and Santa will be coming to town on the top of a fire engine provided by the Indiana Fire Association. The main focus will be on The Jimmy Stewart Museum and its *It's a Wonderful Life in Miniature* exhibition on its second floor. All promotions state that limited tickets for the public viewings are still available.

125

Juniper excuses himself after dessert, explaining that there is still lots of work to do to finalize the production for the viewing the following night, and in less than 10 minutes he's back at the museum testing the completed changes. He knows that he can't get this wrong. He's invested a great deal of time, risked his career, and put his marriage on the line, and there's no turning back.

While testing the swimming George Bailey figure, he receives a call on his wristband. It's Sayre.

"How ya' doing buddy?"

"Doin' fine, I suppose."

"Were you able to work with the figure of Clarence I sent?"

"It was a breeze, just like you said. I really do appreciate you having my back. But I still don't quite get it. One moment we're working together and the next we're not. Are you schizoid, or am I?"

"For now, just try to roll with it. We're working together well, and we have similar goals."

"I'm not too sure of that, John. Yours always seem a little shady."

"I like to win," Sayre says. "Right now I'm betting on you, but you're a wild card. The best thing I can do when playing a wild card is to play it cautiously."

"So we're not friends, and you're using me."

"No, we *are* friends, and I'm using you. But you'll benefit from it. Hope it goes well tomorrow. I read the reviews, and they were great. All my best."

With that, Sayre hangs up.

Juniper tests the George Bailey figure over and over again to see if the character is convincing as he swims with Clarence to the shore. With regard to his own dilemma, he can well envision himself being just what Sayre called him... *a wild card*. But then again, is he truly like Bailey diving into a canal to save a perfect stranger? Is he, too, a person who doesn't possess an ability to love unconditionally? After all, on his own model at the museum, it's Christmas Eve and George Bailey's wife and children are home, while George is contemplating suicide, and then saves the life of someone he doesn't know rather than thinking about the state of his own family if he dies.

He's aware of the parallel with his character, but also knows that his situation isn't really the same as Bailey's. His isn't a life or death struggle.

"So why aren't I with my wife?" Juniper says to himself. "Why'm I here in Indiana instead of back at home in Crestoria saving my marriage? Is my ego really that big? Am I really that unbalanced?"

He watches George Bailey dive in and save Clarence one more time. It's what people want to see... a man rescuing a stranger... without thoughts of remuneration, his own safety, or the future of his own family.

The snow is falling on Bedford Falls.

"If snow is all they care about, then who am I to say they shouldn't have it," says Juniper to himself.

The scene ends with a spotlight on the bridge fading into the darkness and strings of lights lining Bedford Falls' parkway, the only other source of illumination now on the model. A single car, a Model T, skids its way south along Genesee Street and is followed by the light from a single star shining through the snow-filled sky.

Voices rise from speakers placed near the monitors and are heard roughly vocalizing lyrics taken from the final scene of the original film, as the old automobile struggles through tracks forged in the snow by previous cars now back at home, past the near-naked downtown, and aims towards the dark oblivion at the layout's termination.

Should auld acquaintance be forgot
And never brought to mind?
Should auld acquaintance be forgot

And days of auld lang syne?

Juniper's heard the words a hundred times, but has never quite understood their meaning. He speaks the words "Meaning of auld lang syne" into his wristband, and it responds, "Days long since past."

"Ah," he thinks. "How sadly appropriate!"

He turns off the power in the gallery, but instead of heading back to the suite, returns to the bedroom on the first floor of the museum in hopes of sleep, a chance for a better tomorrow, and a pathway back to Leonder.

Chapter Twenty-One
Light One Candle

After a restless night's sleep in the museum's makeshift bedroom, Juniper awakens to the smell of coffee. As he leaves his bed he is surprised to find Faye and Nancy talking quietly and making breakfast on a sandwich grill in another room.

"You're finally awake," says Faye. "It's past 8:00 and we thought you'd be at the model by now. Would you like some breakfast: an egg white omelet, fried kale and grilled tomatoes?"

"Thank you both," he responds, rubbing his eyes. "It's nice of you. I did oversleep, but since I finished about 4:00 AM, I guess it's still early for me."

"We thought you might need a pick-me-up. Today is a big day," says Nancy.

"Yep, and I think we're ready," Juniper replies.

"By the way," says Faye. "Those packages over there are for you. They arrived by drone this morning before we got here."

Juniper looks over at four small packing crates. They are numbered, with a catalogue envelope taped to the top of crate number one. He knows who sent them, but can't imagine what they contain, since as far as he's concerned, the layout is as ready as it can possibly be for the day's events.

"Some of your technical people have already arrived upstairs," says Faye. "They apparently got here a little after 6:00."

Juniper walks to the packages and opens the white envelope that's simply titled "Juniper."

Good morning, my friend!

I assume you've had a difficult night's sleep, but I am sure you are ready for the guests to arrive today. I will be one of them, as I made a reservation earlier for a private tour at 4:00 PM. I hear that Poppy Hager will be coming from 60 Minutes at the same time, as well as a few other special guests who weren't at the preview last Friday. You'll be surprised how word has gotten around.

The contents of this crate and the others are gifts to you from me. I am sure they will serve you well and are to be used at the conclusion of each performance. The instructions for them are simple. As with some of the other figures recently sent, they are pre-programmed. All you need to do is remove the clear tab that activates the battery and place them at various parts of Genesee Street in inconspicuous places. They will know what to do from that point on and need no further instructions. Batteries last for about six days of activity so, as with the other figures, be sure to change batteries every two weeks. I have enclosed several packets of our latest glass batteries as well. One more thing: at the conclusion of your presentation (I assume that the characters from the film will be singing Auld Lang Syne*) make sure that the snow continues to fall and the lights of the town remain activated.*

I am very much looking forward to viewing the model in person. Your documenting video team has shared footage with me throughout the process, but that isn't the same as seeing it in person. As you know, I am quite a critic of model construction. I most certainly wish you the best of luck for what you have done. I also hope that it brings you great satisfaction.

– John

Juniper opens the first crate. It is filled with the same style of gray boxes that housed previous figures delivered from Sayre. Inside, enclosed in a debossed foam liner, is the miniature figure of a middle-aged woman in a long coat, hat and scarf. She is rendered in shades of black and white, consistent with the grayscale scheme of the model. In one hand she is holding a song book.

With Faye's and Nancy's help, Juniper opens the remaining boxes to find other figures, also dressed for winter and holding a book in one hand. It doesn't take long for him to figure out that they are carolers. The ten include three young children: two girls and one boy.

The second crate contains similar boxes, housing figures also dressed for winter, but in various styles of dress. Several characters appear ready for a walk. One is accompanied by a dog on a leash, and two children are dressed for winter play in snow boots, ear muffs and tassled hats, boxed together with small white beads, which Juniper assumes are snowballs.

When he finishes his breakfast, Faye and Nancy carry the boxes upstairs to the second floor. Knowing that his instructions provide little information except for him to place the figures out of view on Genesee Street, he selects locations behind buildings, in doorways, and behind trees and bushes at various distances from the main thoroughfare. Having no real idea of what will happen, but imagining the possibilities, Juniper fast-forwards the controlling drive to the presentation's final scene.

As the Model T leaves Genesee Street and the monitors fade to black with the chorus of *Auld Lang Syne*, there is a slight pause and then a single soprano voice comes through the speakers as a female appears from the doorway of the drug store singing *a capella*:

God rest ye merry gentlemen
Let nothing you dismay
Remember Christ our Savior
Was born on Christmas Day

The voice of a baritone follows an older figure walking down Jefferson Street to the corner of Bailey's Building and Loan to join in the song:

To save us all from Satan's pow'r
When we were gone astray
Oh tidings of comfort and joy
Comfort and joy
Oh tidings of comfort and joy

Two young boys find their way from the south end of town to begin the next verse:

In Bethlehem, in Israel
This blessed Babe was born
And laid within a manger
Upon this blessed morn
The which His Mother Mary
Did nothing take in scorn
Oh tidings of comfort and joy
Comfort and joy
Oh tidings of comfort and joy

Several characters enter the scene from various directions, stopping some paces away from the small chorus to listen, while two African-Americans, one a bass and the other a contralto, walk from the courthouse to form a second row of carolers:

Fear not then, said the Angel
Let nothing you affright
This day is born a Savior
Of a pure Virgin bright
To free all those who trust in Him
From Satan's pow'r and might
Oh tidings of comfort and joy
Comfort and joy
Oh tidings of comfort and joy

The figure walking the dog steps into the scene and stops to listen, not far from others who have stopped, while the four remaining singers, two men and two women, come into view and stand next to the previous two, joining the chorus for its final refrain.

When the carol ends, instead of the scene going dark, a second song is begun by the full choir. It's Peter Yarrow's touching Hebrew song, "Light One Candle," written about the Maccabee children slaughtered in Judea in 168 BC. It concludes with the refrain voiced only by the two young boys:

Don't let the light go out!
Don't let the light go out!
Don't let the light go out!

The lights of the town remain on as the chorus members return to their hidden origins.

Juniper, Faye and Nancy are speechless. All have tears in their eyes knowing that the concluding performances most certainly will provide emotional impact to the segment's presentation.

Juniper repositions some of the latest characters, but besides his slight adjustments, all he now has to do is wait for the first guests to arrive.

Chapter Twenty-Two
A Success?

Philadelphia Street is filled with vehicles and people by 2:00 PM as crowds assemble for the parade that begins at 5:00. The largest gathering is at the 9th Street entrance to The Jimmy Stewart Museum. Juniper and his crew fill their time by testing and retesting the lighting, monitors and other electronics of the model. Faye, Nancy, museum employees and volunteers gather in the third floor galleries reviewing their instructions and the adjustments they might need to make if the crowd becomes larger. The documentary filmmakers continue to capture footage of the work performed on the model while also conducting the interviews with the people awaiting entry.

"I've come from Maryland to see this," says one man about 25 years old. "From what I've read, the technology is amazing. I'm not a huge fan of the film *It's a Wonderful Life*, but I enjoy model railroading and this seems like the ultimate experience for people like me. I sure hope I can get in to see it today."

"I flew here from California two days ago, and actually got a preferred ticket to the event because I'm a part-time reporter for the *LA Weekly*. I love classic films, and *IAWL* is one of my favorites. From what I've read, this exhibit's over the top."

"My name's Jerry Mulligan, and I've lived here in Indiana for thirty years and have never visited The Jimmy Stewart Museum, but this I had to see. I love model railroading and build my own miniature buildings in HO-scale. I've heard the technology is crazy, and can't wait to see the robotic people. I wish I had heard about it sooner. I would have loved to participate. Is there any place I can sign up here, today?"

The people in the crowd have come from near and far, with each having a reason to be one of the first to witness the performance. With safety a primary concern for the museum, the staff has created an entrance and exit plan that utilizes an old service elevator for those with handicaps. But it's an old building, not built for crowds.

When asked by the documentary film crew whether they were prepared for the number of people expected, Faye didn't flinch in providing a response.

"We're open today, tomorrow and every day after that, except Christmas Day. If they miss it today, they can come earlier tomorrow. It's a public event, and we're not used to this many people. By next year we'll be able to handle the crowds much better."

"But you knew this would happen, didn't you?" asks the interviewer.

"We had no idea what to expect when we started out," answers Faye. "As with any you launch, you can only hope for publicity and attendance. Many times we've had only a few cars and one busload of people show up for a special guest star. As we followed the progress, we started to get the feeling that was possible, but even as recently as last Friday, we were doubtful about attendance. We're going to do the best we can to keep people happy and entertained. We have a puppet show on the third floor, a satellite exhibit of our museum at the other end of Philadelphia Street, and we have the *It's a Wonderful Life* film with its original soundtrack recorded by the London Symphony Orchestra showing at the Indiana Theater down the street.

"Our own Nancy Boyle, Indiana's Director of Tourism, has scheduled a Jimmy Stewart look-alike contest at 3:00 today in the Fisher Auditorium of IUP, and Eric Cowell, son of Simon Cowell, the late television personality, is conducting a Jimmy Stewart impersonation competition at Miller Stadium at 7:00.

"Christmas tree growers, having had a disastrous ten years after the blight, are offering trees from their first growth of a new variety of Douglas fir at cut-your-own prices for trees up to eight feet in height.

"Besides that, all of our stores are open until 10:00 tonight with special discounts. The Jimmy Stewart Museum will also be open until 10:00, including our new exhibit. That's about the best we can do!"

At 2:00, Poppy Hager shows up with her crew to film an interview with Juniper at 4:00. The schedule is tight, and her crew sets up a mini studio on the first floor of the museum. Having attended the preview, she knows some of what to expect, but will also need new footage of the third-floor layout. With the documentary film crew already present, there are too many cameras on the second floor, so Poppy agrees to have them provide raw footage of both the room in its current state, as well as with the crowds inside. That way Poppy's crew can use both of their cameras to capture the interviews.

At 3:45, Poppy's assistant lets Juniper and his makeup person know that they are ready to shoot, and ushers the man of the hour back to the first floor, and into the makeshift studio. Poppy and Juniper talk a bit as she tells him what she knows and doesn't know about his mission. He brings her up to date on most of what has happened since the previous Friday night. Poppy explains that the interview will be edited back at the *60 Minutes* studio, and that their talk will primarily concern his professional life, and the collaboration between him and his team. The director indicates that the crew will start filming in two minutes.

Poppy: Indiana, Pennsylvania, isn't often a major destination for national news teams, and The Jimmy Stewart Museum hasn't been in the headlines for many years. From what we gather, the museum has been struggling to survive as Indiana's favorite son, Jimmy Stewart, passed away more than sixty years ago. What made you decide to launch a project in a town of such little note and a museum with little money?

Juniper: There were several opportunities for such a venture, one in Pittsburgh that fell through, but that inspired Faye Gunther and Nancy Boyle to seek me out. My real job is a fact checker for AI. I assure that information used by AI is as accurate as possible, so that decisions aren't made on a whim. I'm good at my job, but my passions are model railroading and classic films. Pittsburgh has plenty of history, but so does Indiana, and more than that, it is the birthplace of Jimmy Stewart, a favorite of mine. More than that, Indiana demonstrated a need for my work, and permitted me to develop the program I believed would be best for them.

Poppy: Judging from the size of the crowd outside, and the praise the exhibit is getting from the press, I would say that you have probably exceeded your goals.

Juniper: Not necessarily. We discovered during our preview that our exhibit hall is too small, and that some people may not want to watch a complete showing of the two-hour-plus program in a crowded room. Fortunately, we are only showing a few segments today, each taking 20 minutes at the most.

Poppy: I have heard that the full exhibition will be ready for the holidays next year.

Juniper: That's the plan, but meanwhile we have had to make some adjustments to the segment shown last Saturday.

Poppy: Are you ready?

Juniper: With the help of the CEO of M-Bots, John Sayre, we're ready.

Poppy: And who is this Mr. Sayre?

Juniper: Like me, he's a model railroad enthusiast, but also a designer of miniature robots, a main part of the attraction we've created.

Poppy: I heard there were some disagreements early on between you and Sayre.

Juniper: You heard right, Poppy. But we've gone beyond those and he has become my greatest ally in getting where we are in the production thus far.

Poppy: What is your personal mission... or objective... of mounting the exhibition? Fame? Fortune? Personal?

Juniper: I think that my desires have changed over time, but I believe that some people crave the *doing* of certain tasks, whether it's acting, painting, music, sports, mathematics or construction. From Lindburgh's transatlantic flight into adulthood Jimmy Stewart wanted to fly, and he did so for most of his life. He studied architecture, but found a passion in entertaining people and acting. He succeeded in both. He believed in America, so he went to war to battle the enemy using his skills as a pilot and an actor, and he lived to tell about it. His qualities are evident in the characters he played, first in *Mr. Smith Goes to Washington,* and then as George Bailey in *It's a Wonderful Life.* Stewart became identified with his parts in those films because as a person he understood that there are many forks in the road, and whichever one you take, you must own it.

Like George Bailey, we sometimes need help in making decisions. Clarence, the angel in *It's a Wonderful Life*, was George Bailey's mirror. I have yet to determine mine. And although I thought I knew my direction, I most likely do not.

Poppy: I don't understand, Juniper. You are poised for many possible successes.

Juniper: But I'm also, right now, plagued by the possibility of a very great failure.

Poppy: How so?

Juniper: It's personal, Poppy. Let's just say that by aiming for everything I want, I may lose all that I have.

Poppy: Is there a way to change that outcome?

Juniper: I don't know, but I wish there really was a Clarence to help me.

Poppy: Getting back to the exhibition, where do you see it going down the road?

Juniper: First, the blending of the entire film with the model has to be completed. Without that, the project is fluff and of no significant value.

Second, I believe the county needs a larger venue for people to experience it the way it should be experienced.

Third, I believe that ultimately the exhibition, like all others, will prove to be a fad, but also a stepping stone for future exhibitions, thus making Indiana County and The Jimmy Stewart Museum an essential link from the virtual world of today to the more tactile world of tomorrow.

Poppy: And by that you mean?

Juniper: Most of what has been built on the model has been the result of people using skills that in recent years have become devalued. The team of craftsmen who constructed the buildings and scenery for the exhibit did it for the love of the task, and the opportunity to be part of something greater than themselves. They have, as of yet, received no money for their work, and most don't care.

This project couldn't have been built without them. It also couldn't have been done without a sense of satisfaction gained by the work they were doing. Standing in line today are many who will come through the doors for the first time to see their completed work. That is their reward, and then they must get back to work to finish the task for the following year. If this brings business to the Indiana area, and spawns an industry for people who can build model houses for the pleasure of people in great cities who will pay for their work, so be it. If not, the time was not wasted, since we all have gained a sense of purpose from the doing.

Poppy: Thank you for your interview, Juniper. We at *60 Minutes* all wish you the best and congratulate you on your accomplishment.

Chapter Twenty-Three
Redemption

As the line of visitors grows longer as it rounds the Philadelphia and 9th Street corner and continues north to Oak Street, Juniper's anxiety mounts concerning the museum's ability to accommodate the crowd. Overlying his fear of failure is the sadness he feels when thinking of possibly losing Leonder. She hasn't been in touch with him since returning to Crestoria, and he doubts his ability to repair their marriage, an issue independent of any possible success from his year-long endeavor.

For the moment, he waits on the sofa in his makeshift apartment at the museum, every now and then getting up to peek through the blinds at the ever-lengthening line of expectant viewers.

At 4:30 there's a knock on the door, and Juniper gets up to open it. When it's only halfway open, he sees the face of John Sayre smiling broadly. He's carrying a magnum of champagne with a big gold bow attached to its neck.

"Hi, stranger!" says Sayre enthusiastically.

"John, I knew you were coming, but I almost didn't recognize you," Juniper says while awkwardly trying to hug the man he's met only once before in person.

"Save your hugs, Juniper," Sayre says, using the bottle as a shield. I have someone with me you might prefer to hug rather than me." At which point he moves away from the door and Leonder appears.

"Leonder! You've come. I didn't know. I hadn't heard..."

"Stop it, Juniper!" responds Leonder with an awkward smile. "John called and told me he was flying out and that if I would like to come along, he had room on his shuttle. I'm here, and despite everything I'm proud of you, Juniper. We have our issues, and I don't know whether we can work them out, or how, but today isn't the time to go into that. Today is your day, and I'm glad I can be here."

Faye arrives from her fourth-floor office to tell Juniper that he needs to get ready, as they are about to open the doors to the museum. "People are already waiting upstairs, as well as on the upper level."

"Excuse me while I change my shirt," says Juniper to Leonder and Sayre. "I haven't rested well for the past several nights."

"Besides being a bit rumpled, you look fine to me," observes Sayre.

With a pressed shirt on, Juniper rejoins Leonder and Sayre and they climb the stairs to the second-floor gallery, where they are immediately greeted with applause by a far larger assembly than the 25 expected by Juniper.

Faye hushes the crowd and says, "Juniper, as you can see, these are just some of the people who have helped you with the task of building, landscaping and populating the model. They won't be staying for the reveal, but they did want to be here to thank you for enabling them to work with you on the project. Many more are on the third and fourth floors, and will be coming down soon to wish you well and to thank you for including them in your venture."

Juniper knows some of the people gathered in the gallery, but many others introduce themselves as they shake his hand or pat him on the back.

"I'm Dennis," says one offering his hand. "I built 347 trees, and these are my brothers, Dave and Frank. Together we made 1,000."

"I'm Silo," says another further back in the crowd. "I topped 240 trees, and my friends and their wives made 1,736 altogether."

Faye tries to simplify the introductions.

"Who here was responsible for the buildings?" she asks.

"We were!" answers a man at the other end of the room. "Great plans, by the way! I made seven of the buildings on Genesee Street, including the pop-up facades in George's nightmare. Mike, Stan, Grit and Bo built 14 more."

"I built the bridge," calls a man on the far left.

"Me and my girlfriends created the display boxes for Gower's Drugstore and Potter's office," calls another woman Juniper's never seen.

"They're magnificent," Juniper answers. "No one even told me where they came from until I asked, and I'm sorry if I didn't write to thank you."

"We were glad to do them, and can do more, if you like."

"Me too!" is shouted by a chorus of women who just came down the stairs.

"We did Mary's hall and living room where George and Mary kissed."

"A group of the guys upstairs created the diorama of Philadelphia Street," says one of the ladies.

A man whom Juniper recognizes reaches forward and shakes his hand. He's one of the landscape artists from the borough who's been working with Juniper nearly every night.

"My wife barely recognizes me," he says with a chuckle. "I leave at six in the morning to repair trucks and don't get home until she's asleep. Been that way throughout. Overall, I think it's been better for our marriage."

Several men and women laugh at that, and nod their heads in agreement.

"We don't want to occupy your time, Juniper," says another man in the crowd. "We just want to let you know that you've been great to work with. I don't get a lot of praise at my day job, but the great note you sent me about the construction of Ma Bailey's house and mansion lifted my spirits. From what I gather, you sent notes to most all of us."

"Except for the ladies with the display boxes," responds Juniper ruefully.

Overwhelmed by the warm reception, Juniper answers questions for several minutes. "You've given generously of your time and skills. It's not I who should be thanked, but instead every one of you. I have thought many nights before finally falling off to sleep that there are so many of you who have sacrificed in helping with the project with little to gain. Somehow, I believe you'll all be rewarded for your efforts with more than my thanks."

"Don't worry about it," shouts another man. "We're on board until the completion of your project!"

Faye ushers the guests out of the gallery to make room for more members of the crew, as well as the first in line awaiting the show. Juniper's asked by Faye to say a few words before the official opening and clips a microphone onto his lapel. She then walks outside to the steps leading to the main entrance of the museum. Philadelphia Street is filled, but audio speakers on light poles normally used for traffic announcements are patched into the mics worn by Faye and Juniper.

Faye begins the introduction. "The Tourist Bureau, the Chamber of Commerce, the Indiana Business Association and the Board of Directors of The Jimmy Stewart Museum are proud to begin a new chapter in the legacy of Jimmy Stewart, and of Frank Capra's 1946 film *It's a Wonderful Life*. The man responsible for this moment, Juniper Blakley, has accomplished a remarkable feat, which, although not complete, will over time alter the future for our county. Like Capra, Juniper Blakley has taken a dream and turned it into a reality that will benefit many of us living in Indiana. At this point, we don't know entirely where that dream will lead us, but as witnessed by the press and the turnout today, we can imagine some of what might spring from his imagination, dedication and tenacity.

"There have already been conversations about creating a new facility for the display of *It's a Wonderful Life in Miniature*, and perhaps also creating a number of retail businesses that will provide visitors with a small-town experience typified by Indiana and Bedford Falls in the 1930s and 1940s, minus the hardships.

"John Sayre, the CEO of M-Bots, the firm responsible for the miniature figures in our display, has already been receiving proposals from cities around the world for something similar to the experience Juniper is introducing today.

"I was informed this afternoon by Mr. Sayre that those of you who have contributed your skills, time and handiwork to the project will be among the first to be considered for contracts that he and Juniper might propose in the future, thus bringing good-paying jobs to our county, as well as recognition of the creative talents and skills of the many in our community who have often been undervalued and neglected by companies seeking people with scholastic and academic backgrounds when hiring.

"So without further ado, I introduce Juniper Blakely, aka our own 2060 version of George Bailey."

Juniper clears his throat, and takes Faye's place on the steps of the museum.

"I have learned a lot since beginning this project. I've learned what it means to truly work with others. As a fact checker in my real job, I have always worked independently, but for this project I had to trust in the skills of many people I didn't know, as well as others with motivations which I didn't understand. I may have had goals I wanted to accomplish, but I failed to recognize that without dedicated and talented people helping me, I was just any other man with an impossible dream.

"I was asked earlier in the day by *60 Minutes* reporter Poppy Hager what my motivation was as I began this journey. I believe that at first it was money, freedom, success and fame – in that order.

"To get the job started, I had to give up thoughts of money, since I was asking those working for me to take nothing, or less than they deserved, in return for their efforts. There was no way for me to benefit from the task with so many earning nothing.

"Freedom was the next thing I lost, in that I was tied to the project and a deadline of my own making that occupied me completely, even to extent of damaging my relationship with my wife, the woman I adore.

"Over time, I had no hopes of success and could only see failure as I witnessed the confusion of people trying to make sense of my project. Each day I pushed on, trying to merge the film with the model as I was documented throwing fits and swearing at myself and my stupidity in taking on the project.

"Only recently did I discover just how fleeting fame can be, in that at one moment I am viewed a hero, while the next moment I am reduced to a crumbling pile of refuse, doomed by my own ego, and my failure to anticipate what comes next, as I try to comply with the ever increasing demands of the modern world.

"What was left for me was humility, something I often seemed to have little of. But as I stand here today and look out at each of you, I understand that anything I've gained is from your *giving*, and not from my *doing*.

"At the close of the film *It's a Wonderful Life*, George Bailey's given a note by Clarence, written on the first page of the book *Tom Sawyer*, by Mark Twain. Its meaning is simple, but maybe not as simple as it seems. My friend John Sayre passed me a copy as I stepped out here to speak to you. It says, 'Dear George: – Remember no man is a failure who has friends. Thanks for the wings! Love, Clarence.'

"As I stand here, the first part of the message is clearer than ever to me. Friendships and family are at the core of success and without them there can be little happiness. The second line, written by Clarence, provides the

146

clue to what it takes for us all to become wiser. In real-world terms, Clarence got his wings by having George save him from certain death. He knows that George Bailey's a good man, and has always been there to help others. But, like many of us, George lost his way, and needed a little help to get back on track.

"Right now, I need to pause and get *my* life back on track. So I will be disappearing from Indiana for a while and returning home to California. I wish you all a Merry Christmas, and know that the New Year will be full of promise for the great people of Indiana County."

With that surprise announcement, Juniper returns to the first floor apartment followed by Leonder and John Sayre, neither of whom had expected such a complete turnabout in Juniper's behavior.

Leonder and Sayre pause as Juniper enters his bedroom.

"Does he know what he's doing?" Leonder whispers to Sayre.

"I don't think he cares. He doesn't want to lose you."

"But this is extreme," marvels Leonder.

"Sometimes it takes extreme measures to keep what you know you need."

"I never would have thought..."

"Ah!" says Sayre.

"Did you know he planned to return with us tomorrow?" whispers Leonder.

"I do now," answers Sayre.

Chapter Twenty-Four
Interlude

The mood of Indiana on the evening after Thanksgiving can only be compared with Mardi Gras, a Super Bowl, or the expressive joy of South Philly residents during the New Year's Day Mummers Parade.

Santa is set to arrive from the west on Philadelphia Street atop a 1957 Seagrave Pumper recently purchased and modified to include the logo of the Indiana Fire Association emblazoned on its side. Stores will remain open until 10:00 PM and restaurants have installed propane heaters outdoors for customers willing to brave the chill of late November while drinking coffee, cocoa, cocktails and craft beers. Nancy Boyle had promoted a costume theme to fit the pre-war and WWII era, and county residents have spent weeks searching through family trunks, attics and basements for World War II uniforms, front-buttoned dresses, fishtail trousers, cloches, fedoras, pocket watches, long gloves and other accessories from the 1930s and '40s.

The line into the museum remains long nearing closing time and Faye and Nancy distribute free passes for the next day's viewing to those left waiting. "Come early," Faye urges, with most visitors understanding the capacity problem and the unexpected size of the crowd. Those who made it through the line to the exhibit encourage others who have not yet entered, by praising the display.

"Magnificent! Never seen anything like it!"

"Can't wait to return!"

"Be sure to look around the model for the surprises. There's a figure of a man changing a tire in the snow. His wife's actually helping him. It's f@*%ing unbelievable!"

Meanwhile, after spending some quiet time in his makeshift bedroom, Juniper opens the door and joins Leonder and Sayre in the common area of the museum's first floor.

"Let's sneak out and go to the suite and enjoy the champagne there, John," Juniper says with a conspiratorial smile on his face. "We have the condo until Sunday. Can you stay till then?'"

"I suppose I can," replies Sayre, not knowing what to expect from Juniper, who seems to have awakened from a trance.

"How about you, Leonder. Can you stay until then?" Sayre asks.

"Why not? I haven't anything scheduled."

"That's great," says Juniper. "When you return, do you mind if I come along on your shuttle with you?"

"Will you be able to?" asks Leonder. "Aren't there things you must wrap up... people to meet and greet?"

"I've already met with most of them. I intended to come home for the holidays anyway, so Sunday's as good a time as any."

"That sounds nice," says Leonder.

"I'll have to speak with Faye before leaving, and you and I have a few things to discuss, John, but other than that, let's celebrate! We can pick up some takeout if the lines aren't too long, and if you don't mind picking it up, John? I'm reluctant to be seen right now. In fact, I've blocked all calls for the night."

"No problem," answers Sayre.

"Let's head out of the basement entrance to the parking lot in back. The old elevator's still in the rear, and I don't believe they're using it except for emergencies.

"Fine with me," responds Sayre.

The three sneak surreptitiously past the line and head off to the suite. Before they arrive, Sayre takes a detour back to a sushi place he passed on their way, and lets Juniper and Leonder know that he'll meet them shortly with dinner.

With Sayre gone, Juniper and Leonder are alone together. She decides it's an appropriate time to confront Juniper.

"Okay, Juniper," she begins, " So, what's with your mood?"

"I don't think I have a mood right now," says Juniper.

"Come on. I know you inside and out, and I don't know what's gotten into your head, but something's going on."

"If you're referring to the speech I gave, it was long past due."

"But why today? You've apparently succeeded in every way you'd hoped, and now you're just walking away."

"I'm not walking away, Leonder. If you heard me, I'm still going to run the project, just not from here. I have more important things to take care of right now."

"You mean our marriage."

"Yes, our marriage. I've had a lot of time to think about you and me over the past several days. I've always been proud that I can get more done than most people. I'm focused on deadlines, and conscientious about obligations and duties. But it seems that I have also been neglectful, single minded, self-absorbed and derelict in my affection, and insensitive to your needs. You've also been worried that I've been depending too much on the success of this *dream*, and am ignoring reality. I now believe you may be right.

"From my viewpoint, I've chosen my life over yours, because I've believed my approach to be more correct than yours in just about everything involving the two of us. I've looked at the way you've handled your life and wondered, 'Doesn't she understand what I'm trying to do? Why can't she share my vision? Maybe she just doesn't care about what I need.' Whereas you've been thinking and saying the same about me.

"Therefore, I have two choices: one is to move forward and lose you to my ego, or two is to change my thinking and consider you first before continuing on a path that will divide us forever. What I thought I knew, but have only recently realized, is that you're the most important thing to me in the world, and all of this nonsense surrounding me is not my life. You are my life."

"That's a beautiful statement, Juniper, but I'm well aware of who you are, and I don't believe you'll ever be content catering to my needs and ignoring your own."

"Then let's see what happens over the next month or so, and see if we can merge our lives together, rather than letting circumstances pull us apart. I'm willing to try, if you are."

"What about your obligations here and to all these people who are counting on you?"

"As I said, I'm not abandoning them. I just can't have them as my first priority right now. Most of them are good at their jobs and are prepared to run with the project, including Sayre. My priority is to see if, and how, we can rebuild our relationship. One thing I've learned about life here in Indiana is that the pace is slower than in Crestoria, and the people are friendlier, once you get to know them. Life is simpler, more relaxed and, despite the project,

I've had more time to think."

"Would you like to live here?" asks Leonder.

"I honestly don't know. But now is not the time to consider a move. Now is the time for me to get my priorities in order. In a month or two, maybe we can address changes in our life moving forward."

At this point in the conversation, Sayre shows up with the sushi, and Leonder gets plates ready and opens the champagne. After it's poured, Sayre proposes a toast:

"I choose to borrow the words of Harry Bailey when he showed up at George's house near the end of *It's a Wonderful Life*. Today, after seeing all of the people praising you and your project, I offer a toast to you, Juniper Blakely, 'the richest man in town!'"

Leonder, somewhat stunned, pauses and then clinks her glass with those of her husband and Sayre, and downs its contents in one long swallow.

Worn out from the day's events, Juniper excuses himself and lets Sayre and Leonder know that the suite has two bedrooms and that they should stay the night in the suite. He, however will be having two early morning meetings with staff members, so he will be returning to his apartment at the museum.

He offers no further explanation, but says goodnight before leaving.

Chapter Twenty-Five
The Tryst

The next day, Juniper wakes up early, showers and goes over details with Faye and the crew about maintaining and operating the model. Many people have called about tickets, and the volunteers at the museum have discouraged them from stopping in without reservations, especially this weekend, instead directing them to *jimmy.org* for ordering tickets. Families of workers involved with the project have been given a priority over the general public, since there is just not enough available time or space to accommodate everyone.

Meanwhile, the documentary film crew has captured hours of footage, much of it featuring vignettes recently added into the model that most people don't notice as they attempt to follow the storyline split between the layout and monitors. In order for them to photograph children, parents must sign an approval sheet, but it's worth it to catch the smiles on young faces responding to the humorous side stories missed by parents, such as a figure of a man who, after using an outhouse, trails toilet paper behind him as he wanders back to his cabin.

Once Juniper is sure that all is well at the museum, he contacts Sayre, still at the suite, and asks him if he's ever been to Fallingwater, the historic house built in the 1930s for Edgar and Liliane Kaufmann and designed by Frank Lloyd Wright. Sayre says he that he's never been there and calls across the suite's living room to Leonder, who answers that she hasn't been there either. Juniper calls up the corporate car and asks it to pick them all up at the suite in twenty minutes. The drive is about 50 miles, and the trio arrives before lunchtime with the car letting them off at mid-level parking. Leonder is immediately struck by the integration of natural materials, topography and the structural design of the building that creates the illusion of the house floating above the landscape. She is also fascinated with Wright's postmodern details that transcend the era in which it was built, and enable it to appear as if constructed yesterday rather than 130 years ago.

"It's a magnificent setting, and beautiful art," Leonder remarks to both men. "It's no wonder Wright has become such an icon. Pure genius!"

"It's no longer easy to find places to build over streams and waterfalls like Wright did," says Juniper. "Most all of the land like this has been turned over to the state or purchased by it. There's similar land for purchase near Buttermilk Falls in Indiana that contains a small waterfall and creek, but opportunities for building homes organically are becoming even rarer as safety codes interfere with the creative process."

The three visitors stop in the café for coffee and a snack before continuing on their tour, which takes them through rooms influenced by Wright's design sense as well as his architecture style that extracts dramatic views of the surrounding woods, falls, boulders and the creek bed beneath.

As it's still early when they leave Fallingwater, Juniper suggests a side-trip to Polymath Park, another Wright creation just a short ride north in the town of Acme.

Polymath is a collection of four individual homes placed in one location, all of which are available for overnight stays. The restaurant is open until 6:00 PM on Sundays, so rather than returning immediately to Indiana, the three decide to head off to the park and an early dinner before the return trip.

"I'm impressed," says Leonder.

"Me too," agrees Sayre. "When did you have time to come here, Juniper, with the schedule you've maintained?"

"It hasn't been all work," answers Juniper. "Whenever I have a free moment the transport is there for me, and I've gotten familiar with the area. Pennsylvania is a beautiful state."

Throughout the journey Juniper had avoided all talk of the exhibition, and has refrained from any mention of it long after they've returned to the suite in which Leonder and Juniper apparently will be sharing the same bed. Leonder wonders whether Juniper will use the opportunity to initiate sex, and is surprised at his forthrightness when broaching the subject.

"Due to our recent discussions, I'm not sure how you feel about getting together with me tonight, or ever," says Juniper matter-of-factly as they start the process of brushing teeth, washing up and turning down the bed. "Today was a great respite from our issues, but I know it doesn't change anything concerning our relationship. If you'd like to make love, we can, but I want you to know that I completely understand if you don't want to."

"This is out of context, Juniper, but I have a question for you."

"Go ahead, ask whatever you want."

"Why, when I came to Indiana before, didn't you take me to the places we went today?"

"Unfortunately, I didn't have time," answers Juniper. " I also didn't know about either place until Faye introduced them to me recently."

"You also said that you had no time to find a house for us to live in?"

"I don't want to justify my actions, but my time was restricted by the tasks at hand."

"But today you had time?"

"Yes, because I told all of Indiana I was returning home for an extended leave."

"Did it have to be that you either had to stay or leave?"

"Maybe, and maybe not. I don't really know, Leonder. I'm very conscious of time, and know by instinct what must be done and when it must be done. You know that about me. But I now have committed time to you – as much as you need from me."

"Do you choose to do that, Juniper?"

"It isn't about choice. I need to do that in order to impress upon you how important you are to me."

"What about a time in the future when you get tired of impressing me? Will you just walk away without a thought?"

"I hope to God that I never do that. But I can promise you that I'll give our marriage my best effort."

"Then please, let's have sex tonight. It's been too long."

"My pleasure, but let's not be too loud. The walls are thin, and Sayre's a light sleeper."

Chapter Twenty-Six
Juniper's Troubling Dream

*O*n a clear morning in March following Juniper and Leonder's abrupt *return to Crestoria after the public November opening of* It's a Wonderful Life in Miniature, *Leonder asks her husband if he'd take a shuttle ride with her without asking any questions. He accommodates her, as he's been doing for the past three months, and in five hours the couple lands 50 yards from Jimmy Stewart's Cessna at the airport that bears the actor's name. It is Juniper's first visit to Indiana after his unexpected exit, but the driverless car that spirited him from place to place during his tenure at the museum arrives, as if summoned, the moment they deplane. He's expecting to be taken to the museum, but instead the couple heads south to a spot he's never been to before, a wilderness of late winter, home to black bears, turkeys, falcons, bobcats, and cottontails.*

"Where are we?" he asks Leonder as they turn up a dirt trail off Route 22 near the small town of Florence.

"We're near a favorite spot of Mr. Rogers, Indiana County's second favorite son," says Leonder. "We're heading for Buttermilk Falls, a place made famous by the children's show host more than 70 years ago as he told tales of spending summers here with his grandfather, a wealthy industrialist who owned the land. The falls are further down the road, but a smaller falls is just around the bend."

"And why're we here, Leonder?"

"It's a bit of a surprise and somewhat of a bribe," answers Leonder.

"How so?"

"We are going to own this little piece of heaven."

"Can we afford it?"

"You'll be able to. I have inside information."

As they approach what appears to be a work site, Leonder confesses to her husband the conspiracy she's been involved in with John Sayre, a plot that started shortly after the holidays ended. Her version of the story is that she was contacted by Sayre to discuss Juniper's future, and Sayre told her that the head of city planning for the city of Pittsburgh had been in conversation with him regarding the abandoned project Juniper had presented for the region.

Sayre's version goes something like this: The head of city planning said, "We've tried to communicate with Mr. Blakely, but he won't answer our calls. We know that he's been working with you on the Wonderful Life project in Indiana, and we thought you might be able to encourage him to reconsider working with us... along with you and M-Bots, of course."

Sayre knows that Juniper is sometimes as bullheaded about not working as he is about having his own way, and he knows his friend's main reason for not responding – his promise to his wife. So Sayre figures he will go directly to the source, Leonder, and see how the couple has been handling Juniper's self-imposed exile.

"He's doing well, John," says Leonder. "We're both doing well. But honestly, I don't know how he does it. It doesn't seem to be an act. He's not angry, and

he doesn't appear frustrated. He speaks with Faye frequently, and keeps the project moving along, but without Juniper totally engaged, who knows what will happen."

"I've spoken to Faye," replies Sayre. "She says that some progress has been made, and they know they need a larger space to house the model. But enthusiasm is waning by some of the supporters. Some feel that the preview segments are enough and that there's no reason to take the concept to a conclusion.

"Let me get to the meat of what I'd like to see happen, Leonder. And let's see if it works for you. We probably both agree that Juniper will never change his ways, and maybe his love for you will carry him along for a while, but your love for Juniper has to kick in at some point."

"John! I never..."

"Let me finish. There's no doubt that you need something in your life beyond being an accessory to Juniper's success, so I have a proposal. What if you had a chance to come east and build your own home nearer to the project? What if you get to call all of the shots for your and Juniper's personal life and shape it the way you want? Could you then let Juniper continue the work he's started both on the Indiana project, and the Pittsburgh project? Would you? Will you? If I foot the bill?"

"You're trying to bribe me, John!"

"Come on, Leonder. We both know this isn't the way it should end for Juniper. He's driven by demons neither of us understand, but he's proven himself to you. No one can change his mind without receiving your blessing. And I'll guarantee you this, Leonder, that if he comes east, he won't fail.

"Faye told me that the town was thinking of building a Bijou Theatre, off the old railway trail in the northern outskirts of the borough. It's the place on the map near where Juniper placed Bedford Falls on the model. The theater would be constructed using plans already drawn up by Knowlton & Gidday. It's big enough inside to house the entire layout, plus there's room for expansion and all of the space needed for other events as well. They even proposed the possibility *of building a real Genesee Street and lining it with stores and restaurants. Thus far, it's just an idea that won't see the light of day without Juniper."*

Sayre continues, "For myself, I want to segue the modeling of animated figures away from M-Bots, and I've been toying with the idea of a partnership with Juniper in the new entity. For working purposes I'm calling it "Wonderful Life Miniatures." It would specialize in all manner of figurines for modelers, theatrical displays, films and corporate events. Juniper would be in charge of planning and development, and he would be based near the location of the two pilot projects and have the freedom to expand the business any way he desires, if he chooses to do it.

"So think about it, Leonder. In the meantime I'm sending you some photos of a property that you might like to see. It looks a little like Fallingwater, without the house. We could call it a down payment on a dream, if you choose to accept it."

"It's too much for me to comprehend at the moment, John. I'm a little put off by your assumptions, but I understand your reasoning. Let me think it over and I'll get back to you."

Leonder wavers between enthusiasm for the offer and annoyance at the effrontery of Sayre's evaluation of her. Since Juniper's return home, her own life hasn't changed much, and she's been contemplating having a child if all things go well with her marriage. The truth is that she's already stopped using birth control since Juniper had been away for so long, and hasn't gone back on it since their sex life has never been much of a priority for either of them.

She's even asked Juniper if he'd like to start a family, and he said he hasn't thought much about it, but if she'd like to, he's game. She doesn't think his response is particularly inspired or committed, but what the hell.

So, a few days after Sayre's contact with her, she calls him back.

"I've seen the photos," she begins. "It's a beautiful setting."

"Is this Leonder?" Sayre says, smiling to himself.

"Yes, of course it's Leonder. Who did you think it was?"

"*Have you made a decision?*"

"*Yes.*"

"*Have you spoken to Juniper about it?*"

"*No.*"

"*Then, what have you decided?*"

"*I'll take your offer.*"

"*A smart move.*"

By the time Juniper is invited by his wife to see the plot of land, Leonder and Sayre have agreed to sign a contract with the landowner. Leonder begins working with the architects Knowlton & Gidday on sketches, and she already has an offer on their pod in Crestoria.

"We're meant to be together, Juniper. You've proven your love for me, and now I'll have the freedom to do what I want to do, while you'll be free to create whatever you can imagine. And we'll be together."

Juniper isn't all that sure about the terms of this agreement, but, if anything, he thinks he may have won a battle without putting up a fight. While some would say said he's been too passive, others would maintain that he's being smart.

"So I can go back to work, Leonder?" he asks.

"I'll be waiting for you every night until you come home," answers Leonder.

"Then I have things to discuss with Sayre and with Faye. Are we going back home now, or staying here tonight?"

"The borough has arranged a suite for us, as well as a dinner at Boxer's."

" I should be happy," thinks Juniper. "Everything's working out for the best."

Chapter Twenty-Seven

The Confrontation

Juniper and Leonder enjoy their romantic encounter, but during the night he's awakened by an unsettling dream, and isn't quite himself the next morning, prior to their flight back to Crestoria. Although he knows he's doing the right thing by leaving the project, he can't seem to shake his uneasy reaction to the dream.

"Are you okay?" asks Leonder, noticing Juniper's mood.

"I didn't sleep well," he responds, forcing a smile as he looks into her eyes to determine any changes in his wife since the night before.

"I know this must be difficult for you right now. You know you don't have to leave here this moment for my sake," she says with sincerity.

The car arrives at the entrance to the suite on schedule and the shuttle's waiting for them when they reach the airport. Less than five hours later they're back in California.

Juniper spends the remainder of the day cleaning track on his model railroad, as Leonder works on a series of tiles commissioned by the community center in Crestoria. No one from Indiana contacts Juniper, which indicates that they aren't having any problems managing the movement of people at the museum, or encountering any technical difficulties with the electronics synchronizing the model's systems.

Leonder explains her project to Juniper. "The tiles are made of local clay embedded with dried wild flowers picked along local roadways. The flowers require a resin protectorate to keep them from losing their vivacity as well as preventing the color in the petals from bleeding onto the clay background prior to glazing."

Juniper's impressed with the technology of her media and the complex geometric patterns she's created. He asks about other projects she has in the works.

"Nothing right now, Juniper. But after seeing Fallingwater and Polymath Park, I have some ideas I'd like to explore."

The couple discusses little more before going to bed. Juniper is looking forward to returning to the strict morning routine he abandoned after leaving California.

At 6:00 AM he gets a call from Faye, where it's already 9:00. "There's a problem with the operating system. The program had just gone through two full cycles and then stopped working. We have visitors waiting and the tech guys are here but no one knows how to fix it."

"Did they shut down the main computer, log back in and try to restart the application?"

"Yes, they say they did that, but nothing."

"How about the automatic retrieval system? Did they copy the app over and open it following the restart?"

"Let me put Ed on. He'll know better than I," says Faye.

"Hi, Ed, this is Juniper. You're having problems, I hear."

"Yes! Right after the second cycle this morning the system locked up and we can't get it to restart. We shut everything down, and relaunched the app, but nothing."

"There's a backup system that's fully loaded. Do you have access to it?"

"I never knew there was one on site. Where's it located?"

"It's hardwired in for situations like this. In fact, we have two. If you're logged into the main system, click on the icon called 'Jezebel.'"

"Jezebel?"

"Yep."

"Okay, I found it."

"Normally it should kick right in on its own, so you'll have to call the programmers and see what's wrong, but you should be able to manually start the backup system by typing in the user name 'Jezebel,' and the password: 835Philly#!."

"Okay, I'll give it a try; stay with me while I enter the password."

Juniper waits for what seems like minutes, but it's only about 30 seconds.

"Okay, I'm in," says Ed.

"Now just click on the 'Jezebel' icon."

It takes a few minutes, but the monitors come alive with the "It's a Wonderful Life in Miniature" logo on the screen, and Juniper can hear the train whistle growing stronger as the train begins to round the bend toward Bedford Falls.

"Got it!" exclaims Ed.

"You'll need to contact the programmer since the switching system obviously isn't working as it should. You should also check the system every day prior to the start of the performances. The programming company, CompMed, is local.

"The second icon is 'Salome' and the password for that drive is 650Philly#!. If this happens again, CompMed has an additional backup at their location, so they can swap out a faulty one pretty quickly, or can operate the perfomance remotely from their location, if necessary.

"Good luck, Ed!"

"Sorry to interrupt your vacation, but I never got the instructions for the restart."

"They're on the first page of the manual, but when things fail, manuals are the last place most people go to."

―――――――――

Leonder is standing in the doorway, watching her husband as he finishes the call. He doesn't seem upset or nervous. He's almost smiling.

"Juniper!" she says sharply. "This isn't going to work."

"What, our marriage?"

"No dummy, you doing penance and isolating yourself here."

"I work remotely very well, as you can see."

"Yes, but you're also a hands-on kind of guy with multiple talents and abilities. You're not the one who needs to change, I am.

"You're the one who craves work, and you're the one who's destined to lead us into the future. I'm the one who wants a respite from all of the worries and concerns, and I'm the one who should and can support you and help you on your mission."

"You've been supporting me, Leonder, throughout our marriage."

"And maybe that's my problem, and not yours. If you want to know what I want to do, I'll tell you."

"Yes, I do. Go ahead!"

"I'd like to find a house that can be a real home, or build one to fit our needs. I may even want a child, or children, naturally or by adoption. I want to work with people and help them find their happiness, but I have to find myself first. I can handle a majority of the tasks necessary to run a home as well as do my pottery. I can make friends with people..."

"All of that sounds good, if that's what you really want. I know that you're capable, and creative and bring a lot to our marriage. It may just be the time for you to explore your own potential, and do whatever it is you need to do to feel good about yourself...instead of beating yourself up for what you think you aren't and haven't done, or what you think I want you to do. I can't give you a list, but I can help you on your journey, if and when you want me to.

"I'm here with you right now, Leonder, because you've made me realize that my path may have been leading me to a dead end. By finding your own direction, you'll be helping both of us, and I want to share in your journey as much as, or more than, follow my own.

"Does that make sense to you?"

"Very much so, Juniper. So where do we start?"

"You tell me."

"Suppose you stick around here till the end of the holidays, and then you go back and get to work. Sayre told me that he'd like to partner with you. He also said that Pittsburgh still wants you to work on their project."

"When did he tell you that?"

"The other night when you went back to that slum you were living in at the museum. So how 'bout if I start to look for a home for us back east, one where I can have a pottery studio and you a barn for your railroad hobby, if and when you have time for it."

"And you don't mind if I go back to work, Leonder? And you'll move anywhere to be with me?"

"Not anywhere, but *most* anywhere, Juniper. All I need is a little encouragement from time to time to make me know I'm needed. You may not understand it, but sometimes encouragement is more valuable than love."

"I'll have to keep that in mind, Leonder. I always thought they went hand in hand."

"I've thought about it a lot over the past few weeks and I see how I've placed a burden on you by not defining my needs. What I've come up with is that love is often selfish and an expression of one's own feelings for another, while encouragement is selfless, and an honest response to the needs and desires of the person one cares for, even if they conflict with one's own desires. I appreciate your willingness to sacrifice your future for me, but what I find more romantic and honorable is your willingness to accept me for who I am, and to enable me to define myself as the person I really choose to be."

Chapter Twenty-Eight
Back to Business

O n January 3, 2061, Juniper heads back to Indiana to begin the updates to the model layout. Leonder takes the shuttle with him to scout out rental houses and land available for purchase in the Indiana area.

Faye has made a preliminary tally of the receipts from the ticket sales since the public opening, and though many tickets were comped, the exhibition still brought in nearly $125,000. The museum's sale of cards, shirts and memorabilia rose from $12,000 in November to $38,000 in December, hotel occupancy in the borough alone grew by 48% that same month, and retail and restaurant sales increased by 72% – all significant increases.

Juniper presents his findings at a meeting of all of the groups involved with the project.

"The main source of income has been from what the Tourist Bureau has gleaned from the hotel tax, and from private and public contributions, and that is $5.5 million. The largest expenditures were for the services of the architectural firm of Knowlton & Gidday, and M-Bot for their animated figures. These costs exceeded $3.7 million. Since the job is yet to be completed, each entity is settling for $2.4 million to be paid within 60 days, and the remainder paid, along with additional costs, after the production's completed. The computer programming, lighting and modeling cost an additional $1.5 million, while the trees, bladder control system, landscaping, snow creation and evacuation system and material costs total $130,000. I will be paid $70,000 for my time to date, and $320,000 will be divided between all of the craftsmen involved with the construction of the structures and display boxes."

Juniper anticipates that it will take between $3.5 million and $4 million to complete the project and an annual budget of $80,000 to operate and maintain the layout from the beginning of November to the middle of January. Some think that the model should be on permanent display, but that would require the creation of a dedicated facility with parking and a permanent staff to manage, modify and keep the model operating on a year-round basis.

Wyatt Jenkins, a local developer, had acquired from his father twenty wooded acres located about a half-mile north of the borough to the east of the trail once occupied by the Indiana spur line. When asked about its availability, he agreed to sell the acreage for the price of the timber cut from the land, along with obtaining part ownership of any structures to be built there.

The proposed plan is to create an event venue that can house the *It's a Wonderful Life in Miniature* project, and to allow for its expansion as well as the possible development of shops, restaurants and other businesses surrounding it. The architecture style would be adapted from the Bijou Theatre plans as created by Knowlton & Gidday for the miniature town of

Bedford Falls.

"Won't this venture take business away from the borough?" asks one of the members of the Borough Council.

"There's always the possibility of that," answers Nancy Boyle. "But as long as we have no hotels built on this acreage, I don't think this will be an issue."

"Then what will happen to the existing space used for the display on the second floor of the museum?" asks a board member of the museum.

Faye answers, "We need the extra space for a larger, more modern theater, and I would like to expand on the display box concept to include interiors from other Stewart films. Currently, with all that's happening on the second floor, the boxes get lost on the walls of the exhibition space."

"How would visitors get to this new location?" inquires another board member.

"We think there are several modes of access including walking; riding bikes or other motorless vehicles from the information center on Philadelphia Street; by car from 6th Street and Rt. 954; or by shuttle bus, perhaps designed like an old passenger train, from 9th Street to Rt. 954."

At this point Juniper jumps back into the conversation. "The main thing is that we assure finalization of the complete program for display by November of this year. It's been built in modular form, so it can be taken apart and reassembled at any point. Over the next nine months there's a lot to be done. My wife is looking for a home for us so we can be closer to the project. We like this area, and it's not far from Pittsburgh and another project I may possibly have in the works."

"That's great for you, Juniper," says Alex, a member of the Business Association. "But will the Pittsburgh project make ours seem irrelevant?"

"That's a good question," answers Juniper. "The Pittsburgh project is different. It's about real history. Indiana's is about fantasy. When I first met Faye and Nancy I investigated the history of your area, and found out about its association with the coal industry that lasted over a century. As the concept developed, I realized that your connection with Jimmy Stewart and his role in the making of *It's a Wonderful Life* were much greater attractions than the coal industry.

"What I suggested for Indiana County and the Stewart Museum was a model based on *It's a Wonderful Life,* but one that could also expand to embrace and promote films by actors and directors who worked with Stewart.

"Alfred Hitchcock made more than 50 films in his lifetime, and Stewart and Cary Grant both starred separately in four of the director's films, yet Stewart and Grant only made one together, *The Philadelphia Story.* There's no reason why the eight Hitchcock films couldn't be packaged together for a festival in Indiana and shown in the theater here, or perhaps on the second floor of the not-yet-built Bijou.

"Stewart and Henry Fonda were close friends from an early age but parted ways over politics. In 1970, during the latter part of both of their careers, they made one film, *The Cheyenne Social Club,* together. Although it wasn't their finest work, it reunited them and created a lasting connection. There's no reason why The Jimmy Stewart Museum couldn't capitalize on the bond between the two actors to feature a festival of Fonda films.

"Getting back to the Pittsburgh project: it will explore the city's legacy as a transportation hub that provided access to the midwest and western states after the Pennsylvania Railroad connected to it. By 1882 it became the largest railroad and transportation enterprise in the world.

"So the answer to your question, Alex, is 'No!' Your project is one-of-a-kind, and the premise for it is built on five elements unique to Indiana, the first one being that you already have a movie museum here, one that's recently created a presentation format that exists nowhere else in the world. Second is that Indiana was the hometown of one of the most popular actors of the 20th century. Third, that actor, James Maitand Stewart, was a man of impeccable character and is as remembered for his sense of community, good deeds and heroism as he is for his fame as an actor. Fourth, Stewart was the leading star in the film *It's a Wonderful Life,* the most beloved holiday film in American history, and played a role that represented a man with conflicts between what he wants to achieve and the wellbeing of others. The final element is that Jimmy Stewart's entire life symbolizes the possibility of the rise to fame for every person, and is the ultimate American success story.

"No place I know of has a better story than you have. And right now, you're positioned to take it as far as you choose, keeping in mind that you are also responsible for maintaining the heritage and values of your area, so as not to turn Indiana into a theme park, or sideshow."

By the second week of February, Leonder has found a small rental house west of the borough on West Pike Road, and has begun to look for some land on which to possibly build a permanent home. Wyatt Jenkins tells her about land near a public park at Buttermilk Falls, a spot on a ravine that overlooks a creek and a 30-foot waterfall surrounded by boulders, rocks and natural trails that lead down to a pond in a valley. After hearing about it, she contacts Juniper and asks him to visit it with her.

Upon arriving at the site, Juniper thinks back to his dream the night before leaving Indiana for Crestoria, and the bribe proposed in it by Sayre to Leonder to encourage Juniper to get back to work. This place seems much the same, but it's not exactly as in the dream, and he's sure that Sayre has had nothing to do with his wife finding it.

Leonder rattles off a few ideas she has for their future home, and asks Juniper what he thinks of the property.

"It's beautiful, Leonder. Truly magical. I do have to say that I believe I've seen this before, but can't really tell you when or how. If you love it, let's see if we can afford to buy it. Then it's yours to play with."

On the way back to town, Juniper wonders more about Sayre and his own strange dream, and attempts to make sense of it all. He ponders whether Leonder is sly enough to have manipulated him into getting what she's ultimately wanted. Was Sayre involved in this complicated plot? Is he, himself, truly happy about Leonder's discovery of this place?

This brings his thoughts back to the beginning of the adventure, and his goal of merging his various passions into a single reality. In such a short period of time, it doesn't seem possible that what's developed could actually have happened. Thinking back to his proposals to build an enormous model railroad almost anywhere in the United States, he never could have anticipated the results he's achieved. There were far more obstacles that he overcame, than chances he had for success.

Leonder is still talking about the property as they reach their rented residence. Tomorrow he plans to tackle the scene of George's rescue of his brother from the sledding accident in the pond. If George hadn't lived, Harry would never have become a war hero. If Juniper hadn't dreamed of building the world's largest model railroad, Leonder might never have found happiness, The Jimmy Stewart Museum might have faded into a memory, and he might have continued to check facts for AI until his early retirement and anonymity.

"I guess that's the way dreams work," he thinks to himself, as Leonder continues to talk about her plans of building a living room over the falls just like the Kaufmanns did.

"Sounds like a wonderful idea," says Juniper. "In fact it sounds very much like *a wonderful life!*"

Acknowledgments

The dedication of this book to David Wren is the first of my acknowledgments. He first introduced The Jimmy Stewart Museum to me 20 years ago, and since that time I have had the privilege of painting and producing prints for the museum, designing graphics for promotional items and producing two videos, one of which is a biography of Stewart titled "Always Be Nice to People."

The acknowledgment of David as my "Clarence," is only rivaled by my great appreciation for my editor, Manfred Roesler, who has edited my four previous books and worked with me tirelessly to craft this ode to Indiana, Pennsylvania; The Jimmy Stewart Museum; and the classic Frank Capra film, *It's a Wonderful Life*.

At Fred's suggestion, I extracted this story from a larger work in progress, *100 Years from Today*, and am thankful for the assistance of an Indiana friend and colleague, Jeffrey Tobin, for his preliminary narration and guidance on this and other projects yet to be produced.

I must thank my wonderful wife Barbara for her assistance in creating the marketing materials for this book, and for her objective view of the final project.

Finally, I am most fortunate to have my project blessed by Janie McKirgan, the Executive Director of The Jimmy Stewart Museum, whose mission has been to expand the range of experiences offered by the museum and to take it in new directions to promote and augment the relevance of Stewart's films for new generations of viewers.

– George H. Rothacker

September, 2021

About The Jimmy Stewart Museum

The Jimmy Stewart Museum is a real museum dedicated in 1995 to celebrate the films and life of Hollywood legend and World War II pilot James Maitland Stewart. This novel positions the museum ahead in time to the year 2060 when it faces the challenge of decreasing attendance due to the shrinkage of the actor's fan base, and the memory of his works and deeds.

The Jimmy Stewart Museum today is host to more than 6,000 visitors a year, from all 50 states and many countries around the world. The museum consists of six galleries and a vintage 50-seat movie theater. Through posters, letters, costumes, personal mementos and family photos, it explores the history of Stewart's early years, his courageous WWII service and his impressive Hollywood career that is best known for his roles in four Alfred Hitchcock movies, seventeen western films, numerous comedies, and his Academy Award-winning performance in *The Philadelphia Story*.

Over the years, the popularity of the film *It's a Wonderful Life* has made it a holiday classic, loved by people around the world. Stewart's persona has often been merged with that of the IAWL protagonist, George Bailey. Though the two were quite different in many ways, both are symbolic of the American everyman who sometimes must forgo personal success in order to do what he or she believes is morally right.

Much more can be discovered about the films and legacy of Jimmy Stewart at:

jimmy.org

or

The Jimmy Stewart Museum
835 Philadelphia Street
Indiana, Pennsylvania 15701
724-349-6112

The museum is open Monday - Saturday: 10 AM – 4 PM
Sunday: 12 PM – 4 PM

For more information, contact:
curator@jimmy.org

CPSIA information can be obtained
at www.ICGtesting.com
Printed in the USA
BVHW092334021221
623076BV00021B/559

9 781977 246578